"Keep 'Em Pinned Down While I'm Gone!"

She was lying prone, pressed down on the baked soil twenty yards from the mouth of the cavern, behind a thick cluster of yucca. She was not moving and for a moment Longarm thought she'd been badly wounded, perhaps even fatally so. Then she moved, trying to peer back over her shoulder at the cave.

Longarm took his hat off and pushed it beyond the edge of the entrance arch, to draw the attention of the attackers away from her. A scattering of gunfire rattled and puffs of muzzle blast rose here and there among the widely spaced clusters of cactus that provided the only cover on the slope beyond the cave's black opening. Longarm pulled his hat back quickly. In a moment the shooting stopped.

"There are too many of them out there, amigo," El Gato said. "At least ten or a dozen. I know what you're thinking, but is not a good idea. You might get to the woman, but you would never get back, carrying her."

"Maybe . . ."

— **TABOR EVANS** —

LONGARM

AND THE
NEW MEXICO SHOOT-OUT

J
JOVE BOOKS, NEW YORK

LONGARM AND THE NEW MEXICO SHOOT-OUT

A Jove Book/published by arrangement with
the author

PRINTING HISTORY
Jove edition/October 1988

ISBN: 0-515-09758-6

Jove books are published by The Berkley Publishing Group
200 Madison Avenue, New York, New York 10016.
The name "JOVE" and the "J" logo
are trademarks belonging to Jove Publications, Inc.

PRINTED IN THE UNITED STATES OF AMERICA

10 9 8 7 6 5 4 3 2 1

Chapter 1

"No, ma'am," Longarm assured the young woman who stood beside him outside the courthouse door. "You ain't going to have anymore trouble with that Schroeder fellow."

"But the barrister defending him seemed very shrewd," she replied. "And the magistrate only nodded when the barrister said he was going to appeal Schroeder's sentence."

Elaine Courtland's clipped English manner of speech and her use of British terms such as *barrister* instead of *lawyer,* and *magistrate* rather than *judge,* still sounded a bit strange to Longarm, though he'd heard her use them in her testimony on the witness stand.

"I'm quite sure the barrister meant what he said about filing an appeal," she went on. "If I've learned enough about your laws here in the States, that would bring Schroeder to trial a second time, before a different magistrate."

"I'd say you've learned pretty well," Longarm told her. "And you figure he could be set free if he was to be

1

tried by a new judge who might figure things different to this one?"

"It's possible, isn't it? And if the new magistrate did let Schroeder go free on bail, I'm sure he'd be able to find me easily enough. Everyone around Colorado Springs knows where I live. And Schroeder isn't the kind of man to forget that I'm the only one alive now who actually saw him shoot those people in the Franceville Bank."

Longarm's mind flashed back several months in time. He recalled the bloody scene that had met his eyes on the morning he'd walked into the Franceville Bank. Only a short time had passed since Schroeder had staged his holdup, and Longarm had gotten there quickly because of an odd combination of circumstances. The tiny new town of Franceville was located at the edge of the Rocky Mountain foothills only a few miles east of Colorado Springs, where Longarm had been sent by his boss, Chief Marshal Billy Vail, to escort a U.S. district court's escaped prisoner back to Denver.

Longarm had been in the El Paso County sheriff's office at Colorado Springs signing the papers for the prisoner's return when a federal bank examiner with whom he was acquainted had staggered in, almost falling through the door. With his long experience in judging bullet wounds, Longarm had seen at first glance that the man was fatally wounded, and his snap judgment had proved to be accurate.

One of Schroeder's bullets had torn through the examiner's chest and another through his liver. He'd died only a few minutes after reporting the robbery, and Longarm had realized at once that the bank examiner's death had tagged the man's killer as one murderer who'd stand trial in a U.S. district court instead of a state court—when he was caught and arrested.

Sweeping aside the formalities of legal jurisdiction and primary territorial responsibility, Longarm had volunteered to go with the deputy sheriff who was sent to Franceville at once. Instead of following the torturous winding road through the foothills that began just east of Colorado Springs, the deputy had led Longarm in a beeline on a wild cross-country gallop that got them to the scene in a bit more than an hour.

"He took a woman with him," the Franceville Bank's cashier had reported at once when Longarm and the deputy walked into the bank. "Said she'd be his pass to get free if a lawman caught up with him."

"You know who the woman was?" Longarm asked.

"Oh, sure," the cashier had replied. "It was Miz Courtland. She's the English widow woman that lives between here and the Springs in that big cut-rock house up on the slope. She banks here because it's easier for her to get to our bank here than going into—"

"Never mind all that," Longarm snapped. "Just tell me which direction the holdup man took when he rode outa here."

"My guess from the way he was heading is that he was aiming to take the old emigrant wagon road that winds down to the flats and then goes on to La Junta," the cashier replied. "I figure he'd be aiming to hole up—"

"That's all I need to know," Longarm broke in. "I know the lay of the land along that old trace." Turning to the sheriff's deputy he went on. "You stay here and find out all you can about how much that bandit took and how he came to shoot the bank examiner. I'll go after the scoundrel."

3

Knowing as he rode off that he was having to play catch-up with the bank robber, Longarm summoned from his capacious memory the features and course of the familiar road he was traveling. Then he pressed the livery horse to its limit, gambling that the fleeing killer did not know the road as well as he did. He spurred his mount across country at every loop and curve that the little-used wagon trace described.

Longarm splashed across the small creeks that flowed into the Cuchara River before it joined the Purgatoire and melded with it to form the mighty Arkansas. Long stretches of level prairie and a few expanses of downslope lay ahead. On the level land Longarm forced the livery horse to its utmost, but let the animal set its own pace to recover breath and stamina when he reached a downward-slanting section.

Other than that, Longarm slowed his headlong pace only when the tiring horse gave signs of faltering. The sun had begun dropping westward, but still hung high in the sky when he saw the two horses ridden by the fugitive outlaw and the woman he'd taken hostage. They were still a good six or seven miles ahead, a small moving object silhouetted against the yellowing prairie grass.

There was no cover in sight. Longarm had no choice but to keep on, though he knew that once the outlaw looked back he'd be spotted. His quarry was still out of rifle range when the outlaw ahead first noticed that he was being followed. By now Longarm was close enough to the fleeing outlaw and his captive to see the frantic manner in which Schroeder wielded his quirt. He could also tell by the narrowing gap between them that thanks largely to the led horse on which the woman was mounted, the fugitive's horse was dangerously close to

4

being winded, for the animal was not responding to its rider's slashing blows.

Bit by bit the gap between them closed, but there was never a time of more than a moment or two when Schroeder failed to keep the horse ridden by the woman he'd captured between himself and Longarm. Even with the range lessening, Longarm did not intend to risk hitting the captive with a slug intended for the outlaw.

Schroeder had no such restraint; for him Longarm was an open target. Twice as the chase went on across the open prairie the fleeing outlaw twisted in his saddle and raised his rifle to fire. He did not shoulder the gun to aim, but handled it with one hand as though it were a pistol. Longarm did not take the precaution of trying to maneuver either time. He knew that the chance of Schroeder letting off an accurate shot under such circumstances was very small indeed.

Still, the outlaw's efforts to bring him down had given Longarm an idea. He waited until the outlaw turned again to look back, and when he saw Schroeder raise his rifle for another shot, he quickly disengaged his right foot from its stirrup. The outlaw triggered off his shot and Longarm leaned as far back as he could in his saddle while keeping a firm grip on the horn. Then, acting as though the slug had found a mark, he rolled from the saddle and dropped behind the body of his horse.

Longarm clung to his precarious perch as the horse stopped galloping and stood motionless. He was holding himself in place by the iron grip of his left hand on the saddle horn and the one foot that was still jammed into the stirrup. Hanging as he was, hidden behind the horse's body, he could only hope that the animal looked riderless. The horse was standing stock-still, and the only sound that broke the stillness of the prairie air was the huffing of the animal as it recovered its normal rhythm of breathing.

Though Longarm was too combat wise to look over the cantle of his saddle to see how Schroeder was reacting, he knew that his maneuver was working when the distant rhythmic thud of hoofbeats from the outlaw's horse no longer reached his ears. He clung desperately to his sinew-straining crouch as the hoofbeats began again, but this time at a slower tempo. Only a few moments passed before the hoofbeats grew louder. Then Longarm knew that his ruse had a chance of succeeding.

Time seemed to stretch to eternity before the crackling of the dry prairie grass and the muffled thunks from the hooves of the approaching horses reached Longarm's ears. Then a woman's voice overrode the lesser noises.

"I still don't understand why we're going back," she said, "when a few minutes ago we were racing for dear life in the other direction."

"Dammit, woman," Schroeder's raspy, guttural voice replied, "you oughta have brains enough to tell when your horse is going lame. All that running done it in. If we're ever gonna git where we're heading for, we need the horse I shot that fellow off of."

Still maintaining his precarious hold, Longarm waited. He clung to the saddle horn until he heard the squeak of saddle leather as Schroeder dismounted and the outlaw's feet began rustling the high prairie grass. When the rustling told him that the outlaw was within a few feet of the horse, Longarm slid his Colt from its holster and dropped to the ground. He hit rolling and was on his feet with the cold steel of the Colt's muzzle

jammed into Schroeder's throat before the startled outlaw could drop his hand to his gun butt.

"Well, now," he said as he snaked Schroeder's revolver from its holster, "it sorta looks to me like you
ain't heading anyplace but to a date with the hangman's
noose."

Longarm's recollection of Schroeder's capture had
flashed through his memory in the few moments that
passed between the time Elaine Courtland finished
speaking and his reply.

"It ain't likely the judge'd pay a bit of mind to whatever argument that lawyer could put up to get another
trial," he told her. "You can just bet that Schroeder's
going to be in the pen down at Canon City for a long
spell. He'll serve the ninety-nine years the judge gave
him, if he lives long enough."

"You don't think he might escape from the peniten-
tiary?"

"There's only been a few that's managed that,"
Longarm said. "So if I were you, I wouldn't lose any
sleep worrying about him. He won't be bothering you
like he threatened to when we were bringing him back
here."

"It's been very hard for me to forget what he said that
day when he took me prisoner," she admitted. "He
painted some very vivid pictures in my mind with the
threats of what he'd do to me before he killed me."

"Talk's cheap, Mrs. Courtland," Longarm told her.
"Like it was in court today. I guess you noticed how the
lawyers and the judge used the same kind of language."

"I don't think I follow you, Marshal Long," Elaine
Courtland said with a frown.

"Well, that's maybe because you ain't been in as

many courtrooms as I have," Longarm went on. "In my line of work, a man's got to stand up in court and testify about how he came to arrest the crook that's being tried. I reckon you can see why I'd wind up spending a lot of time sitting around listening to lawyers and judges."

"I hadn't thought about that part of your job," she confessed. "The picture I have in my mind of an American federal marshal is a man out on the range on horseback helping someone, the way you helped me by following that man Schroeder after he'd kidnapped me during that bank robbery."

"Oh, I get out and work on cases, too," Longarm said. "And was you to ask me, I'd have to admit I'd rather be outside in a saddle than in a chair waiting in some stuffy courtroom."

"I agree with you, of course. But I can see why you'd have to be at the trial of a man you'd brought in," she said. "And I'm sure you've learned a lot about magistrates and barristers and the law because of that."

"Mostly what I've learned about 'em is that they've all gone to the same kinda school, where they learn how to sling big words around real free."

"I've noticed that myself in England," she agreed, "having had to spend some time talking to both in connection with the family estate I inherited. But I'd much rather—" She broke off as a carryall rounded the corner and the wagoneer reined up in front of the courthouse. Indicating the carryall, she went on. "That's my—don't you call it a rig here, Marshal Long? Do you have a horse that you'll be riding back to your hotel? If you don't, I'll be glad to have my man give you a lift to wherever it is you're going."

"Well, now," Longarm replied, "if it wouldn't take you outa your way too much, I'd be grateful was you to give me a ride down to the Denver & Rio Grande Depot. I figure to catch the night flyer back to Denver when it comes through."

"It won't be a bit out of my way," Elaine said. As she and Longarm started down the courthouse steps she asked, "Which of the hotels by the depot are you stopping at? I'll have the coachman drop you off at its door."

"I checked outa the hotel I've been staying at when court broke up at noon," Longarm told her as they walked toward the carryall. "I could see the trial was going to finish up pretty fast, and I didn't aim to put an extra day's hotel bill on my expense voucher for such a little bit of time."

"Then you don't have anywhere to go until train time!" she said. "And I'll bet you're planning to eat your dinner at one of those dreadful little restaurants down by the station where everything tastes the same."

"That's sorta what I had in mind," Longarm admitted.

"I certainly can't let you do that after you've done so much for me, Marshal Long," she told him. "Since you're not in any hurry, please come and have dinner with me."

"Why, I couldn't just go out to your house and push in for dinner without you having a chance to get it ready," Longarm protested.

"Nonsense!" Elaine told him. "For one thing, I have a cook to prepare dinner. For another, your train doesn't pass through here until midnight, so you can't be in a hurry. I'm not going to take no for an answer."

They'd reached the carryall by now. Longarm extended his hand to Elaine, and though the distance from the curb to the carryall's stirrup step was only a matter of inches, she took it and slid across the center seat to make room for him.

"You'll be doing me a favor by having dinner with me," she went on as Longarm settled down beside her. "I don't enjoy eating alone, and I'll be very glad to have your company."

"If you put it that way, then, I'd be pleased," Longarm replied.

"We'll go home, Steven," Elaine told the wagoneer. "And we aren't in a hurry, so don't press the horse. After the tobacco smoke in that courtroom, I'll be glad to have a breath of fresh air on the way."

Longarm had taken out one of his long thin cigars. When he heard his hostess's remark, he started to return it to his pocket, but she reached across and put her hand on his forearm.

"I don't mind the smoke from a single cigar one bit," she said. "But ten or a dozen cigars going in a small crowded room is another thing entirely. Please, go on and light yours."

Longarm nodded and struck a match by scraping his horn-hard thumbnail across it. As he puffed the cigar into life he glanced idly at the unfolding landscape. They'd reached the outskirts of town now and the character of the street changed quickly. Suddenly it was no longer a street dotted with houses on each side, and instead of grating on gravel, the carryall's wheels rolled almost noiselessly on two well-packed earthen tracks.

"I got to admit, this is a sight better'n sitting on a hard bench in the depot waiting for a train that you know ain't going to come in for another three or four hours," Longarm commented. "And I'll tell you right now, I'm real grateful to you for the favor of inviting me to supper."

"It's you who're doing me a favor," she protested. "I get quite downcast sometimes, living alone as I do now. Believe me, Marshal Long, I'm looking forward to this evening just as much as you seem to be."

Chapter 2

Now that they were in open country, Elaine Courtland was turning her head slowly from side to side, joining Longarm in looking at the vista of small grassed valleys that ran in undulating zigzags away from the road. The shallow valleys cut wide vees up the sides of the broader valley in which Colorado Springs lay and through which the road ran. Off the winding road narrow paths had been beaten to a few widely scattered ranch houses. These were situated on a slope that rose high enough to allow the crests of the Rockies to be seen. Cattle were grazing in places where the shallow saucered valleys dipped and held enough rainwater to encourage the knee-high grasses to grow.

"It's so different, you know," she remarked as though she were replying to a question from Longarm.

"I reckon I don't follow you, ma'am," he said with a frown.

"I don't see how you could," she replied. "I was talking to myself. Even though I've been here for some time, I'm still amazed to find your American West so

13

very different from home. We've nothing to compare to those huge red stones so close to town, the place you call the Garden of the Gods."

"Well, I ain't much on scenery and all such like that, so I don't guess I could say much about it," Longarm told her. "I never was in England, either, so I don't rightly have much to go by when you talk about it."

"Perhaps you'll go to both places someday," Elaine said. "I don't think I'll want to go back to England, though. My husband has been dead for two years now, but home still holds too many memories for me. Besides, I like the freedom of being here in the West."

"You're all by yourself, then?"

"Of course. But Colorado Springs and Denver are handy when I feel the need to get away for a little while."

While they talked, the carryall turned off the road and started up a long graveled drive to an imposing two-story house that stood near the crest of the gentle slope.

"But we're home now," Elaine went on, "and we've plenty of time left before dinner to enjoy a sip of something. You do drink whiskey don't you, Marshal Long?"

"I've been known to," Longarm admitted. "And I don't mind telling you, I'd sure enjoy bending an elbow with you."

"What an odd expression!" She smiled. "I don't believe I've ever heard it before."

"I guess you have some sayings in England that'd sound funny to me," Longarm said as the carryall wheeled into a porte cochere at the side of the house.

With a grating of wheels on gravel the carryall stopped and the driver reined in. He hopped out and offered Longarm a hand, but Longarm shook his head and spanned the gap between the carryall and the steps with one long stride. He turned to offer his hand to Elaine, but the ranch hand was already helping her to alight.

"You won't mind making another trip to town this evening, I'm sure, Steven," she said. "Marshal Long will be taking the late train to Denver."

"I'll be around to pick him up, then," the man said. "It won't bother me a bit."

As the carryall wheeled away, Elaine turned to Longarm and said, "We're here in plenty of time to freshen up a bit. I'll have Charles show you to a spare room that you can use."

"That'll be just fine, Mrs. Courtland," he said with a nod.

"Then we'll have a quiet drink together in my sitting room," she went on. "Charles will show you which door to use when you come to join me. And, Marshal Long, I'm sure that you don't feel any more comfortable being formal than I do. My name is Elaine, and I like it much better than I do Mrs. Courtland."

"Why, sure," he agreed. "Now, I got a sorta nickname that I cotton to more'n I do anything else. It's Longarm."

"How clever!" She smiled. "The long arm of the law! And it suits you so well in another way, as tall as you are. Until later, then—Longarm."

Charles said at once, "If you'll be so kind as to follow me, sir, I'll show you to a room."

Longarm fell in step with Charles as the butler led him up the sweeping curved staircase and along a pleasantly dim, cool hallway lined with doors. Charles opened one of them and bowed, saying, "I'll wait for

15

you here in the hallway, sir, and show you to Madame's room."

"Fine," Longarm said. "It ain't going to take me but a minute."

Stepping through the door, Longarm found himself in a spacious bedroom. A door on one of the side walls stood ajar, and he could see that it was a bathroom. A lavatory stand holding a washbowl and pitcher stood by the wall between the spacious bathtub and toilet. Crossing to the stand he dropped his hat on the chair beside the lavatory. He made quick work of washing his hands and face, reached for his hat, then after a moment of hesitation left it on the chair beside the lavatory.

When he returned to the hall, Charles was waiting patiently. He turned wordlessly and led the way to a second staircase. Following him up the steps, Longarm saw another wide passageway ahead, and as he followed the butler along it he noticed that it had fewer doors. At last they reached a door which stood ajar, and Charles pushed it open a bit wider before turning to Longarm.

"Madame's suite, sir," he said. "She has asked me to invite you to enter and make yourself comfortable. There are liquors on the table, sir. Please select what you wish while you are waiting. And should you need anything further, sir, please ring."

With a bow, the butler retraced his steps down the hall. Longarm watched him for a moment, then stepped inside. The room was furnished with an array of puffy velvet-upholstered divans and chairs, arranged to allow their occupants to look out the wide windows that overlooked the green valley's upslope. Doors were at each end. They were ajar, as had been the one from the hall. Along the back wall stood a long narrow table laden with bottles and glasses.

16

Longarm crossed to the table and scanned the bottles. After he'd spent a moment searching among the array of whiskies, liqueurs, and brandies, he finally spotted the familiar name he'd been seeking. With a satisfied smile he lifted the bottle of Tom Moore from its resting place and pulled the cork. He looked for a shot glass, and after studying the array of tall glasses, stemmed glasses, and tumblers, settled on one of the latter.

He clinked the bottle neck on the glass as he poured and was about to replace the whiskey bottle when Elaine Courtland called, "Charles? Is that you?"

"No, ma'am," Longarm replied. "It's me, Elaine."

"Would you like to come join me?" she asked. "And bring a drink for me when you do."

"Why, sure. What's your fancy?"

"Whatever you're drinking," Elaine answered.

Longarm filled another of the oversized shot glasses with Tom Moore and carried both glasses through the open door from which Elaine's voice had come. He looked around at the room he'd entered. A canopied bed flanked with nightstands filled most of one wall, a dressing table and a chaise longue occupied another. There were a few puff-bottomed chairs scattered about on the deep carpet of the floor. Across from the door by which Longarm had entered another door stood ajar.

Balancing a glass in each hand, Longarm pushed sideways through the door. A wave of moist heat met him and his jaw dropped as he saw Elaine. She was stretched out in the oversized bathtub. A layer of sudsy foam spread over the surface of the bathwater, but the foam was not thick enough to cover the rosy puckered tips of her swelling breasts rising above its surface.

"I'm sure you're not too surprised to hop into the tub

and join me," she said with a smile. "It's the nicest way I can think of to get better acquainted."

"I ain't going to argue about that," Longarm agreed. He handed her one of the glasses of Tom Moore and placed the other on a small table that stood beside the tub. "But I sure wasn't counting on us getting real cozied up so soon."

As he spoke, Longarm levered out of his boots. He laid his gun belt carefully on the table beside his drink, dropped his trousers and kicked his feet free, then shed shirt and balbriggans with one quick shrug of his shoulders.

"Oh, my!" Elaine gasped as Longarm turned to face her. "I was sure you'd be a lot of man, but I must say..."

What she felt she must say went unspoken as Longarm stepped into the wide, deep tub and settled down beside her. As he sank down, the level of the suds-covered water deepened, but Longarm did not need his eyes to find the swelling globes of her breasts and caress them with the tips of his fingers. He felt Elaine's hands on him, feeling and fondling, and bent to kiss her, opening his lips to her questing tongue.

Weightless in the warm water, they lay supine and silent for a short while, lips meeting for long intervals and parting when both were breathless. Their hands were never idle. Longarm continued his caresses of Elaine's soft globes while her hands were constantly busy at his crotch, stroking and squeezing. At last she leaned away from him and looked up, her eyebrows raised inquiringly.

"Are you as ready for me as I am for you?" she asked.

"My way's to let the lady call the tune," Longarm answered.

"Then I say let's sing louder!" Elaine replied, rising to her knees, then standing up and stepping out of the tub. Longarm followed her. They stood side by side on the soft, thick bathmat for a moment. Longarm's erection had vanished as he stood up and the air stirred by their movements swept around them.

Elaine was bending over the pile of thick, soft towels on the tub-side table. She turned and looked at him, then picked up the glasses of Tom Moore, still untouched. She handed one to Longarm before raising her own. They touched the rims of the glasses together, and though Longarm downed his drink in a single swallow, Elaine took only a sip or two from her glass.

"Oh, my!" she exclaimed. "That's stronger than I remembered. I'm going to need what you call a chaser here!"

Dropping to her knees in front of Longarm, she began rubbing his flaccid shaft on her cheeks and neck. He needed no long stimulus. His erection began immediately, but before it could peak Elaine had engulfed him completely. Longarm did not move while she continued her soft caresses, and he swelled and grew in response. At last she released him and leaned back to look up at him. Her cheeks were flushed and her eyes glowed, while the rosettes of her bulging breasts were pinkly pebbled, their tips protruding.

"Now!" she exclaimed. "Hurry, Longarm!"

Longarm bent to pick her up, but Elaine grasped his arms and pulled him toward her.

"Now!" she repeated. "The mat's as soft as the bed! Hurry, Longarm! Can't you see I'm burning up?"

Longarm's urgency was no less than hers. He

dropped to his knees and pulled her to him, and Elaine squirmed beneath him as she clasped her legs around his thighs and placed him for the prolonged penetrating thrust that brought a cry of pleasure from deep in her throat.

Then Longarm began stroking in a long, measured rhythm. For a moment or two Elaine lay supine, accepting his plunges with moans of satisfaction. As he continued and showed no signs of slackening, the moans rippling from her throat grew louder, and now her hips were rising in rhythm with his thrusts. Suddenly her body jerked and quivered and the rhythm of her responses became ragged jerks, then a convulsive trembling shook her as she cried out loudly and went limp.

Longarm did not break the rhythm of his stroking, but kept his deep penetrations going as before. Elaine lay quiescent for a moment or two, accepting his thrusts but not responding. Then she sighed a long, broken, jerky sigh, and Longarm felt her body growing taut beneath him once more.

As the minutes ticked away and Longarm continued his deep drives, Elaine broke her silence again. Short whimpers bubbled from her throat and became moans, and these grew into small formless shrieks as her hips began gyrating again, but now she brought them upward with such force that their bodies met with loud fleshy smacks.

Her small formless shrieks were almost constant now, and as Longarm speeded the tempo of his thrusts the shrieks merged into a single continuing cry that pulsed in rhythm with Longarm's lusty penetrations. Elaine's pulsing cries began to break, and her writhings were constant now. Longarm was stroking faster, the climax he'd been delaying for such a long period beginning to assert itself.

Elaine's writhings had mounted now into uncontrollable jerky spasms. By this time Longarm was pounding again, his lunges like trip-hammers, and when Elaine's final shrieks broke from her throat, he speeded up for one last deep plunge. As Elaine's last ecstatic cry broke from her throat he also reached his climax. Longarm pressed himself to her writhing, shuddering form until his spastic waves ebbed and died away. Then he relaxed on her soft body while Elaine's subsiding cries of satisfaction sounded in his ears.

It was Elaine who broke the silence first. "If I wasn't sure what happened to me, I wouldn't believe it," she said softly, whispering in Longarm's ear. "And all I can think of is having it happen again after we've had supper and rested for a little while. You don't really have to catch that train tonight, do you?"

"Looks like I got to," Longarm replied. "But it's early yet. We don't have to move, except maybe to the next room. And was I you, I wouldn't worry too much about supper. There's some things I enjoy a lot more than I do a good meal."

"Well, now, Billy, I'm downright sorry," Longarm told Vail. He was sitting in his favorite chair in the chief marshal's private office. "But things happened down to Colorado Springs, things I hadn't figured on."

"I don't mind you giving the sheriff down in El Paso County a hand, but all you had to do was to send me a wire that you wouldn't be back until today," Vail said.

"You wouldn't've gotten it till today anyhow," Longarm pointed out. "And I didn't figure on that freight train I had to hitch a ride on getting sidetracked in Sedalia and standing half the night on that siding."

"How'd you happen to miss the night flyer?" Vail asked.

"Just like I told you, Billy. I just fell asleep and missed it."

"Knowing you, I've got a pretty good idea you weren't in bed by yourself." Vail grinned.

Longarm knew better than to comment on his boss's remark. Instead, he said quickly, "Well, from what you told me a minute ago, that big muckety-muck from the Indian Bureau didn't let you know he was going to come up here or that he'd be wanting me for a job."

"I suppose that's one way of looking at it," Vail said after a thoughtful moment of silence. "But after I'd told him you were due to be here when the office opened today, I felt like a damned fool when half the morning had passed and you still hadn't shown up."

"And you say he won't tell you what he wants me to do?"

"No, dammit, he won't!" the chief marshal snapped. "I don't mind telling you, I just about fell out of my chair when he came in here yesterday and said Judge Parker had recommended you for a special Indian Bureau assignment."

"Sounds like to me you're as mad at him as you are at me," Longarm suggested as he scraped the head of a match and lighted the long thin cigar that he'd taken out of his vest pocket while Vail was talking.

For a moment the chief marshal was silent, and the anger had gone from his voice when he said, "I suppose I am at that. Dammit, I'm the chief marshal here in the Denver district! Who does that pencil pusher think he is, telling me that I can't sit in with you and him while he's explaining this special job to you?"

22

"Now, that's one I can't answer for you, Billy," Longarm said. "But—" He broke off as a tapping sounded on the office door and the pink-cheeked young clerk stuck his head inside.

"Mr. Harrington, that man from the Indian Bureau, is back again, Chief Vail. He wants to know about Deputy Long."

"Show him in," Vail grumbled.

"Well, it looks like I'm going to get connected up with that fellow now," Longarm remarked. "So maybe both of us are about to find out what this is all about."

Chapter 3

Longarm was quick to recognize the stance of authority in Harrington's manner when the Indian Bureau man came into the office. It was shown first when he brushed through the door immediately, without waiting for the young clerk to move aside. There was power in the newcomer's cold black eyes as he flicked them over Vail with a quick glance and turned to survey Longarm. Authority was also obvious in the hard set of his jaw and in his manner of speech after he'd completed his quick stock-taking and turned back to address Vail.

"This is the man you couldn't find yesterday, Vail?" he asked. His words came out flatly, staccato, without inflection.

"That's right," Vail said. "Deputy Custis Long."

"Good," Harrington replied. "At least you were right about him showing up today. Now, I'll need the use of your office for a quarter of an hour, Vail. Perhaps a bit more. I'm sure you have some other place where you can work temporarily, while I talk to Long. If you'll gather up any papers you need and close the door after you, I'll be obliged. I'll have your clerk call you when I'm through talking to Long."

Vail was staring at Harrington with his mouth open before the newcomer finished speaking. It was one of the few times Longarm had seen his chief startled to the point of speechlessness. For a moment he thought Vail was going to protest Harrington's abrupt manner, but the chief marshal recovered his poise quickly.

"I'm sure you'll let me know the result of your talk," Vail said as he stood up. His voice matched Harrington's in flatness, but did not show quite the same firm edge of authority. He went to the door, stepped through it, and disappeared.

"Close the door, Long," Harrington said at once. He was moving towards Vail's paper-piled desk as he spoke.

"I don't reckon I'll need to lock it," Longarm remarked, stepping unhurriedly to the office door. He pushed it closed.

"No. I doubt that we'll be interrupted," Harrington replied. "And sit down, Long. This is likely to take a while."

Longarm returned to the red, morocco-leather-upholstered chair in which he'd been sitting when Harrington arrived. He took out one of his long thin cigars and lighted it, aware of the Indian Bureau man's close scrutiny but ignoring it.

"Damned if I'm not beginning to believe you might be able to bring off this job I've come here about," Harrington said at last. "But then, Judge Isaac Parker assured me you could when he recommended that I come here to Denver and talk to you."

"I've helped the judge a time or two," Longarm said

with a nod. He spoke casually, as though responding to a remark about the weather.

"Your chief spoke very highly of you as well," Harrington went on. "And after talking to Judge Parker, I used his direct telegraph wire to Washington and had my aide wire me your service record before I left Little Rock. It seems to confirm the impression I got from Judge Parker."

"Looks like to me you've done an awful lot of checking up on me, Mr. Harrington," Longarm said. "And then you coming here, that's bound to mean you've got some kinda tricky job in mind."

"I suppose you could call it that," Harrington said.

"Then why don't you just trot it out and talk about it?" Longarm asked. "Because it ain't my way to say much of anything until I know what in the hell I'm talking about."

Harrington smiled for the first time since he'd entered the room, but the smile did not lessen his authoritative manner as he replied, "That's just what I'm going to do. But I had to satisfy myself first that you were the man I was looking for."

"Go ahead, then," Longarm invited. "I'm listening."

Settling back into Vail's well-worn chair, Harrington began by saying, "I don't have to ask you how much experience you've had along the Mexican border, Marshal Long. That's on record—though by reading between the lines I've formed a pretty good idea that not everything you did on either side of the Rio Grande was fully reported."

"Maybe I sorta skimmed over one or two things a little bit," Longarm replied. "I never was much good at pen pushing."

Harrington looked across the desk at Longarm. He

said nothing for a moment. In spite of his expressionless face, Longarm could see that he was making a final decision. At last the Indian Bureau man spoke.

"What I'm going to tell you can't be repeated outside of this room, Marshal Long," he said.

Not only the words Harrington had chosen to use, but also the sober overtone in his voice made Longarm sit up straighter. He studied the Indian Bureau head's face as Harrington went on, saying, "To save time for both of us, I'm going to tell you right now that I've thought about this very carefully. I've ruled out telling anybody in the Indian Bureau or the army about it. I've considered the Secret Service, but it's not the outfit it used to be when Allan Pinkerton was in charge of things."

"I reckon you've already got the idea that I ain't much of a flap jaw," Longarm said when Harrington paused. "Go ahead."

"I suppose you've noticed that the Apaches have been a lot more active than usual lately?"

"I'll tell you flat out, Mr. Harrington," Longarm said, "unless I got a case in the Indian Nation or down in Apache country, I don't pay much mind to what the redskins do. If they ain't fighting among themselves, they're usually butting horns with the army."

"You put it very accurately," Harrington commented. "Right now it's Geronimo's bunch and the little tribes led by Nachez who're doing most of the fighting. And it's not all against the army or the whites along the border. Now that Diaz has given them a place to live in Mexico, they're raiding on our side and running back to Mexico where we can't get at them."

Longarm stared for a moment at the Indian Bureau man, then asked, "You figure to send me to Mexico to chase 'em over to our side of the line single-handed?"

"Nothing like that," Harrington said quickly. "Crook's getting the border crossings pretty well controlled now. But the land on our side is much more densely settled now, and the Indians are a lot weaker. However, that's not your problem, Long. It's mine, and I'm dealing with it. What I'm more concerned with than anything else is that the Apaches seem to have an unlimited supply of gunpowder these days. And we can't find out where it's coming from."

"I guess by 'we' you're talking about the army and your outfit, too?" Longarm suggested.

"Of course. But in spite of their trying, the Secret Service hasn't been able to find out anything for the army, and the local Indian agents haven't done any better for my outfit," Harrington confessed. "So I've decided to try something else."

"Meaning that I'm the something else, I take it?"

"I don't think I need to answer that question, Long. If I didn't have you in mind to carry out my plan, we wouldn't be sitting here talking. Denver's quite a bit more than a step away from my office in Washington."

"Suppose we get down to cases, then," Longarm suggested. "You ain't told me much that I don't already know."

"So far, I've been trying to find out just how well you know the territory where you'll be working. Our border with Mexico is something more than a thousand miles long, and the gunpowder the Indians are getting could be leaking across it almost anywhere."

"Now, I ain't trying to show off for you, Mr. Harrington, but you can cut some pretty big slices off of that thousand miles you was just talking about."

"Go ahead," Harrington said when Longarm stopped.

"Tell me what you're thinking of, based on what I've said so far."

Longarm nodded, then said, "Texas has got a pretty good border patrol along the Rio Grande, and the Rangers work hand in glove with it. The way I look at it right this minute, you can chop your thousand miles in half."

"Very true," Harrington agreed. "Go ahead. Your deduction interests me."

"Now, there ain't no Indians I've ever heard about along that little strip where California and Baja come together, so that gets rid of another hundred or so miles."

"I'll grant you that as well."

Longarm went on, saying, "Then what you got left is where Arizona Territory and Mexico butt together, and that little tit that pokes down from New Mexico Territory between the Rio Grande and the Arizona border. Am I still right?"

"I'd be hard put to argue with you, Marshal Long, even though I'm sure that some of the people on my staff in the Bureau wouldn't agree."

"How many of 'em have seen that border country we've been talking about, and know what it's like?" Longarm asked.

"Not many," Harrington admitted. "But you've got to remember there are several hundred men employed by the Indian Bureau. I couldn't possibly know all of them."

"That's as might be"—Longarm nodded—"but it don't mean nothing to what I'm saying. It looks to me like all you need to do is watch the Southern Pacific trains that haul freight close to the border and confiscate any gunpowder that you figure might go to the red-skins."

"My people in the Indian Bureau aren't exactly stupid in our operations, Long," Harrington said. His voice was icy. "We've been doing that for years. Until recently the border tribes that make all the trouble haven't been getting enough gunpowder by railroad freight to load both barrels of a derringer."

"But that's changed lately?" Longarm frowned.

"A few months ago," Harrington replied. "And the amount of gunpowder shipped on the railroad hasn't increased, not even by a few barrels."

"There ain't but one thing that's happened, then," Longarm said. "The gunpowder's coming from some-place else."

"Exactly," the Indian Bureau chief agreed. "There are exactly two hundred and four gunpowder plants in the United States right now. We've checked to find out where they're shipping to, how shipments could've been diverted, and whether their shipments have gotten bigger. I'll guarantee that wherever all that extra powder's coming from, it's not from them."

Longarm was frowning thoughtfully before Harrington finished talking. He said, "Then it's got to be coming out of Mexico."

"Not according to Mexican authorities. We've checked on the factory reports too. They're as concerned as we are. I guess you know that there are a dozen groups down there, all of them trying to toss Diaz out?"

"Sure," Longarm said with a nod. "That ain't been a secret for quite some time."

"You've had enough assignments along the border to know the country down there pretty well," Harrington observed. "You have no wife or other dependents. I've found out a great deal about you, Long, from checking your service record and case reports. Incidentally, I have a very strong suspicion that you've gone a lot deeper into Mexico than regulations authorize."

Longarm made no effort to widen the crack that the Indian Bureau chief had opened. He said, "I guess I got the whole thing straight now. You've picked me out to go down and see if I can find out what your folks or nobody else has."

"You put it very well, Marshal," the Indian Bureau chief said. "But you omitted one key fact."

"I guess you better tell me what I left out, then."

"You won't be going as a United States marshal. You'll be a private citizen traveling on whatever business seems called for in your new situation."

"You mean you're going to fire me from my job here?"

"Your job will be waiting for you if—that is to say, when you get back," Harrington replied quickly.

"Does that mean I'll be paying my own way?"

"Don't worry about money. You'll have all that you need, and no expense account to file."

Engrossed in his talk with the Indian Bureau chief, Longarm had let his cigar go out. He took a match from his vest pocket and flicked his thumbnail across it, relighted the cigar and took a puff or two. He was not in the habit of beating around bushes. His conversational tone did not change when he made his next remark.

"What you've been telling me without coming right out and saying it in so many words is that you want me to be a spy."

"That's a matter of judgment, Marshal Long. I won't agree or disagree with you."

"Suppose I was to say no?" he asked.

"We've never met or had this talk if you say no," Harrington replied. "I'll deny ever having met you and the only thing I'll ask of you is to do the same. But if you'd like some time to think it over—"

Longarm broke into Harrington's reply. "If I took time to study over everything I do, I wouldn't be worth much in this job I got. I'll take you up on your proposition, Mr. Harrington. When do you want me to leave?"

"As soon as possible."

"Would you say tonight'll be soon enough?"

"If you can arrange it, yes. I'll have to arrange for your expense money and sit down with Chief Marshal Vail for a little talk." Harrington was frowning thoughtfully now. "Suppose we meet in my suite at the Brown Palace at, say, four o'clock this afternoon? Will that give you all the time you need?"

"I don't imagine I'll have too much trouble getting ready by then," Longarm said. "And I figure the best place for me to start from is Fort Bliss, so if you'll fix it up with whoever's in charge there to have me a horse and some army rations I can tote easy and not worry about going bad, I'll be obliged."

"You won't have to worry about getting anything you need," Harrington replied. "Just make a list and hand it to me when we sit down together at four."

Longarm nodded. As he went through the door he stopped and suppressed the smile that had begun to ripple across his face. Chief Marshal Vail was sitting at the desk usually occupied by the pink-cheeked young clerk. Vail's face was more than pink, though. His lips were compressed into a straight angry line and his high, balding forehead was wrinkled into a scowl. He looked up and saw Longarm.

"Well, why're you grinning like a Cheshire cat, Long?" he demanded. "I don't see anything worth smiling about in here."

"When you come down to it, I don't either," Longarm said. He did not break stride, but kept walking toward the door that led to the hall. "But maybe you'll feel different when you've finished talking to that Indian Bureau fellow. You see, Billy, I don't work here any longer."

Before Vail could reply, Longarm was out the door and taking long strides toward the stairway.

When Longarm left the Federal Building, he turned down Stout Street to Eighteenth and walked at a leisurely pace until he reached Champa. There he turned east and strolled at the same easy pace to Dan Fields Saloon. The saloon was deserted at this hour of day, between the early-morning eye-opener and the prelunch trade. The barkeep did not have to ask when he saw Longarm enter, but set a bottle of Maryland rye on the polished mahogany. Then he got a good look at Longarm's face and nodded without speaking, then retired to the far end of the bar where he began wiping glasses.

Longarm tossed off his first shot of rye, refilled his glass, and sipped the potent golden liquor slowly. When his small swallows had drained the glass, he set it down, tossed a half-dollar on the bar, and left the salon. He walked several blocks along Champa Street until he came to a small brownstone building that had no windows displaying merchandise and no sign hanging from its facade.

It might have been a private residence except for the small brass plate tacked to the door, which bore the words THEO BRYSON—GUNSMITH. Longarm entered the shop. There were no counters or displays of stock.

Closed wooden cabinets stood neatly aligned along three of its walls, and a wide, deep, cubelike desk with shallow drawers on all four sides took up most of the space in the center of the room.

In the rear, twin carbide reflector lamps concentrated their beams in a single spot over a workbench. A tall man was bending over the top of the bench when Longarm entered, but when he heard the door close the workman turned. He blinked as he pushed a pair of thick-lensed, gold-rimmed spectacles up on his forehead, where they gleamed like a second pair of eyes below a closely cropped thatch of snowy white hair.

"Ah, weel, Longarm," he said. "Come along in. It's been a while tae be sure, since you dropped in last."

"There's just been too many cases of late, Theo," Longarm replied. "But I've just got out of that. And since there might be some times when I'll need a little extra help in what I'm getting into now, I've come to ask your good advice."

Chapter 4

Longarm had walked the length of the shop while he was speaking. Theo extended his hand, as firm and calloused as Longarm's. Longarm shook it warmly.

Theo Bryson stood a half inch or so shorter than Longarm, though if the withering and stooping effects of age had not done their work on his sturdy frame he'd have topped Longarm's height. His grey eyes were clear and sharp; his cheeks—at least the small arcs of skin visible between a set of feathery, white, burnsides whiskers—displayed age lines but no wrinkles. While the palms of his hands had the callouses of a man who'd worked for a long lifetime in the most intractable of metals, their backs bulged with the compensatory muscles gained by mastering the stubbornness of well-tempered steel.

"I've nae seen ye for a mickle o' months," Bryson said. "Hae ye been gone on so many of yer cases, then?"

"Well, I've been away from Denver more than I've been here," Longarm answered. "And every time I get a few days in town and think about stopping by to see you, Billy finds some kind of new case to send me out on."

"Then 'tis good for ye that ye're busy, because that's bad for the evildoers," the gunsmith observed. "And I dinna doot ye'll be going out again soon. I suppose ye've come in because there's trouble wi' one of yer guns that needs seein' to."

"This time you're wrong, Theo," Longarm replied. "My Colt and derringer are both in good shape. But just the same, I've come looking to you for help, or maybe just a bit of advice."

"Ye've ne'er taken a mickle of the advice I've gi'n ye for a' these years we've been friends," Theo said, grinning. "Sae I misdoot ye've changed the noo. Help, that's anither thing. Wha' is yer after needin', Longarm?"

"A year or so ago you mentioned a new kind of gun you were working on. How's the work going by now?"

"Ye're talkin' aboot my self-reloader, I misdoot?" Longarm nodded and the old gunsmith went on. "'Tis a'but finished. Noo I'll be makin' a' the drawin's I'll hae tae send tae get a patent, then find the brass tae build me a plant. Or mayhap I'll sell the patent. I've nae decided the noo."

"You mean you've really made a pistol that'll fire more than a half-dozen rounds and still be small enough for a man to carry and draw fast?"

"Aye. But ye know the mickle a' years I've been trying tae make it. And there's ithers wi' the same idea, Longarm. Sam Colt's drawings tha' he made before he died are open tae all of us the noo. And young Dickie Gatling's hard at work tryin' tae shrink his big self-reloader. Then there's Barnes and Ripley and Claxton

38

and Williams, sae ye can see wha' a crowd an auld man like me's tryin' tae keep up wi'.'"

"But your self-reloader works?" Longarm asked.

"Aye, lad. It'll loose twenty rounds whilst ye're blinkin' an eye, if ye've the muscle tae hold it."

"Could I have a look at it, Theo?"

For a long moment Theo was silent, then he nodded. "We've been friends tae long f'r me tae say ye nay, Longarm. Come along. I'll nae just gi' ye a look. I'll load it and gi' ye a chance tae try it oot."

Going to the big square tier of drawers that dominated the center of his shop, Bryson took a ring of keys from his pocket and selected one. He unlocked a drawer near the bottom of the case and pulled it open. There, nested in fitted compartments lined with green felt, Longarm saw what he took at first glance to be a pair of long narrow strips of blued steel. Then Bryson lifted out one of the pieces and Longarm saw that it was about the thickness of his thumb and shaped like a capital *L*. The second piece was a thin narrow rectangle, half again as long as the old gunsmith's forearm.

Bryson started toward Longarm, fitting the long straight piece into the short end of the L-shaped weapon. Now Longarm could see that the strange-looking object had dark walnut handgrips set on its short side, and a small stubby rectangle stuck out from the bottom of the ell.

"Not meaning to hurt your feelings, Theo, but if that's a pistol, it's the damnedest one I ever did run across," Longarm commented.

"Oh, 'tis a gun, a-richt," the old gunsmith replied. As he spoke, he was joining the two pieces, fitting the long flat rectangle into the stubby end of the L-shaped piece. He held the assembled gun out for Longarm to inspect as he went on. "And 'tis a handful of one, tae be sure, a mickle heavier than I'd like it tae be. But it'll spit out thirty rounds in a wee eye blink, if a mon's got the muscle tae hold it on aim."

"It's damned big for a handgun," Longarm said, frowning.

"Aye," Bryson agreed. "And heavy when it's got a full load. But steel's steel and brass is brass and lead's still the heaviest. 'Tis nae as bad as it looks tae handle, though. Come along, ye'll soon see."

Walking to his workbench, the old gunsmith opened a drawer and filled his capacious pockets with brass-jacketed cartridges. He picked up one of the carbide lamps and handed it to Longarm. Hefting the L-shaped weapon in one hand, he led the way to a curtained door in the side wall of the shop and motioned for Longarm to go first with the lamp.

A short flight of stairs took them into an unfinished basement. At the foot of the stairs a wire hook hung from a nail in one of the floor joists, and Longarm hung the lamp on it. Although loose boards had been laid edge-to-edge to form a floor of sorts, the room had not otherwise been finished. The brick columns that supported the joists were bare of plaster, and the earthen walls still showed the marks of picks and shovels.

Along one end wall sandbags had been piled to form a backstop for target practice. Three or four paper targets were still hanging on the bags, and here and there tiny trickles of sand sifted to the floor now and then. Bryson laid the gun on the floor and busied himself for a few minutes removing the torn targets and replacing them with fresh ones.

While he worked, Longarm hunkered down beside the odd-looking weapon and studied it. The self-reloader was like no other weapon he'd ever seen. It had no cylinder, no hammer spur broke its angular lines, and the trigger was simply a short strip of steel protruding from a slot in the grip. The end of the strip had been ground or filed into a shallow arc. The magazine was twice as long as the barrel assembly, a rectangular tube of blued steel fitted into the bottom of the gun's grip. An elongated slot had been tooled into the top of the barrel just ahead of the trigger; this Longarm took to be the ejector. He was still examining the unusual gun when Bryson finished hanging the fresh targets and came to stand beside him.

" 'Tis nae finished yet, Longarm," he said, sweeping his hand along the barrel of the weapon. " 'Twill need a trigger guard of some sort, and sights. I've been too concerned wi' getting it tae loose a full magazine wi'out jamming tae gie a mickle of mind tae the odds and ends."

"It jams when it shoots fast, then?"

"Och, aye, it does that. Ye'll need tae fire short bursts and be careful the barrel doesna get overhot. Set yer mind tae remember that the magazine holds thirty loads, and all ye need do tae loose the whole lot is tae hold the trigger doon a wee bit o' time."

"Can I fire just one shot if I press the trigger and let it up real quick?"

" 'Tis hard for me tae work my fingers fast enough, but ye've a quicker hand than mine. Three or four rounds is the least I've been able tae loose."

"And where's the hammer? Hidden inside the butt?"

"Aye. 'Tis a fashed-looking weapon, I grant ye, Longarm. But do ye try it the noo and tell me aboot it."

Longarm picked up the gun. It felt strange and clumsy, and the tendency of the long heavy grip to pull the muzzle up was foreign to the feel he got from his familiar single-action Colt. He raised the weapon to eye level and tried to sight along its short barrel, but in spite of his efforts to hold the arc of the barrel on one of the target's bull's-eyes, the weight of the ammunition in its grip caused the muzzle to rise.

"I don't think it'll ever be worth a damn for aimed shooting, Theo," he said at last.

"Try from the hip, then," Theo advised. "I've seen ye hit bull's-eyes wi' your gun down by your belt."

Lowering the weapon, Longarm found that by cradling its barrel in his left hand and turning slightly to one side he could hold the gun securely. He touched the trigger lightly and the result took him by surprise.

A reverberating *rat-a-tat* of gunfire filled the small basement and assaulted his ears while a stream of brass shell cases flew back toward him, peppering his upper arms and chest. The gun seemed to be trying to pull away from him, the barrel tilting upward, and dozens of black torn spots quickly showed on the targets. When Longarm did release the trigger, the basement was suddenly silent while clouds of acrid powder smoke filled the air in looping swirls.

Longarm lowered the gun and turned to Theo. "It sure does eat up shells," he said. Then he peered through the smoke at the targets and went on, saying, "But I got to admit, it spits out a hell of a lot of lead in less time than a man can count."

"Aye. But 'tisn't a weapon for a man like you," Theo told him. " 'Tis a soldier's gun."

"There's been a few times I wouldn't've minded having a gun like this," Longarm admitted. "But you're right. It ain't a thing I'd want, most any time but now."

For a moment the old gunsmith stared unbelievingly,

then he asked, "Did ye say what I thought I heard?"

"I sure did." Longarm nodded. "You see, Theo, I got a new case that I'll be starting out on real soon. From what little bit I know about it, I'm likely to be going up against redskins, and wild ones, at that. I ain't hankering to give 'em a chance to lift my hair."

Theo was silent for a moment, staring into space. "Where's this case likely tae take ye?"

"Now, that's something I'd like to know myself. All I got to go by is that I'll be starting out way over in Arizona Territory, down by the Mexican border."

"And when d'ye go?"

"Real soon, but I ain't exactly sure just when."

"A day, mayhap twa?"

"Something like that," Longarm said, nodding.

"I've nae got anither one just like this, Longarm," Theo said slowly. "But I've got the model I built before it. It's a rougher piece of work, but it shoots as fast, and 'twould take me only a few hours work tae put it in shape. Would ye settle for that one?"

"I would, and be damned glad to get it," Longarm replied.

"Then I'll put a few touches on it, and ye'll be welcome tae use it on this new case of yours. Stop by tonight, late, and I'll hae it ready for ye."

To Longarm's surprise, when he walked into Harrington's room at the Brown Palace, Billy Vail was there. He was sitting at a table in the center of the room and nodded and grinned at Longarm when their eyes met.

"Mr. Harrington's explained the situation to me," Vail said after Harrington had closed the door. "Dammit, Long! That was a real surprise you handed me back at the office. I'd still be put out at you if Mr. Harrington

43

hadn't straightened me out about the job you're going on."

"I guess what I done was sorta outa line, Billy," Longarm admitted. "But it was just a joke, and I didn't look for you to take me so serious."

"This job's not a joking matter, Long," Harrington put in. "There are too many lives depending on you finding out where all that gunpowder the redskins are using comes from."

"I ain't setting out to argue with you, Mr. Harrington," Longarm said. "But there's more good men than I'd like to think about that's been killed on account of they've gone about a job too serious. Now, my job's my job, and I'm sober when I work at it, but I like a laugh as well as the next man when I ain't working."

Harrington opened his mouth and started to reply, but closed it without speaking. He nodded, then said, "Maybe you're right, at that. At least you're still alive and walking around, and I know a lot of sobersides who're pushing up sod."

"I guess there's got to be room for everybody," Longarm agreed. "But I only got one thing to say, Mr. Harrington. You asked me to do this job and I told you I'd take it on. But without meaning no disrespect, I aim to do it my own way."

"Within certain limits, that's what I expect you to do," Harrington replied. "So, let's sit down and get on with our business." As he and Longarm pulled chairs up to form a close group with Billy Vail, Harrington said, "While we're still on the matter of your badge, Long, suppose you hand it over to Chief Marshal Vail right now. If you were to be captured and it's found on you, it might cost you your life."

"It might save it, too," Longarm answered. "Don't

worry about me letting somebody see it. I'll pin it on the inside of my boot top once I get into dangerous country, and the only way anybody's going to get a look at it is if they're pulling my boots off to bury me."

"Since that's your choice, I'll respect it," Harrington told him. "Now, I've got some maps here that I brought with me from Washington."

He opened the large brown manila envelope that lay on the table and unfolded a map. It showed the western tier of states in minute detail, with the borders of Indian reservations outlined in red. Red cross-hatching spanned three large areas along the Mexican border.

"Here are our three biggest trouble spots," he went on, spreading his fingers to place their tips on the three red-accented areas. "If there are any questions you need to ask about them, Long, I'll do my best to answer."

Longarm had been examining the three red-accented areas. One covered the eastern triangle where the Texas border ran north from the Big Bend area to the panhandle, the second enclosed an oval that included the New Mexico–Texas line at the center, and the third, smallest of the three, spanned the Arizona-Mexico border east of Tucson.

"Well, now," Longarm said. "I won't have to put you to no trouble telling me about them places, Mr. Harrington. I've worked cases in all three of 'em, Billy can tell you that."

Vail as well as Longarm had been studying the map. He nodded and said, "That's right. I don't suppose there are many spots along the Rio Grande where you haven't got your feet wet."

Harrington was silent for a moment, then he said, "It looks like Judge Parker was right about you being the man for this job, Long. Why, I've only been close to one of these myself, and two of them are places where the army's till trying to pacify the natives."

"Sure," Longarm said, nodding. He touched the red areas of the map as he spoke. "You got the Mimbreno Apaches here, and the Lipan Apaches here, and the worst of all three of 'em, the Mescalero Apaches, lay claim to the country in this big blob."

"Yes, I'm familiar with the names of the tribes, even if I haven't been to the places where they claim lands," Harrington said. "Well, Long, I'm satisfied that you're the man we've been looking for. Now, what do you need to do your job?"

"First off, I need for you to give me time," Longarm replied unhesitatingly. "You folks that live back east where you got good wagon roads and a lot of railroads ain't got no idea how long it takes for a man out here to get anywhere."

"If you don't object to me giving you my own interpretation of that, what you're telling me is to stay out of your way as much as possible," Harrington offered.

"Well, now. I wasn't going to come right out and say it that way," Longarm said, "but I reckon that's what it comes down to. You ain't in any big hurry, are you?"

"I may not be, but Congress and the President are," the Indian agent replied. "I'll do what I can to make it as easy as possible for you, though. Now, what else?"

"Money," Longarm said promptly. "Enough so's I can travel fast and maybe pass along a little bit to greedy folks that won't talk until they see some cash."

"That shouldn't be too difficult," Harrington said.

"Not if you got the army on your side," Longarm answered back. "There's still a lot of forts in that country I'm heading for, and every one of 'em's got a paymaster."

"Well, the secretary of war is a good friend of mine," Harrington admitted. "I'm sure I can work something out with him."

"You do that, then," Longarm said. "And that's all I can come up with. You give me time and money, and I'll get your job done for you."

"How long will it take you to get ready to start?"

"I only got one thing to take care of," Longarm answered. "And I'll have that done up tonight. Will tomorrow be soon enough to suit you?"

Chapter 5

"You're damned right, Long. I did send a message back to headquarters in Washington that something's gone wrong," Major Dinwoodie said.

"And you figure the Indian Bureau's to blame for whatever it is going wrong?" Longarm asked.

"They're responsible for keeping the damn redskins in hand, Marshal Long," the major answered.

"But when they get outa hand, then it turns into your job to run 'em down and herd 'em back to their reservations. You'd have to know things like where they like to hide and how they get the powder and lead they need."

"Our orders are not to interfere with the Indian Bureau's work unless the Bureau asks for help."

"What about the wild Apaches, like Geronimo and his outfit? Ain't that what you're here to stop?"

"We ought to be here to stop redskins like him before they get started," Dinwoodie replied angrily. "But the Bureau gives the bloodthirsty ones like Geronimo free rein until he starts raiding the settlers, then they come running to us for help. You're not going to find many of us in the army who have any use for the pen pushers back east that're running the Indian Bureau now."

"Well, I ain't going to say yes or no about that, Major," Longarm told the officer. "I wasn't sent here to do but one job, and that's to find out where the redskins are getting all the powder and lead they're using so free."

"We'd like to know that ourselves," Dinwoodie said. "We've cut off all the shipments of powder and lead that the traders used to get from back east, but the Apaches still seem to have all they need."

"And you don't have no ideas about where it's coming from?"

Dinwoodie shook his head. "No. We haven't been able to find out where they're getting it now."

"Well, I'll guarantee that you can't blame the Indian Bureau for it, Major," Longarm said earnestly. "That's why they sent me out here, to find out where Geronimo and Nachez are picking up all their supplies."

"Don't you think we'd be cutting them off if we knew?" Major Dinwoodie asked.

"I ain't arguing about that, Major," Longarm protested. "I'm just trying to get some ideas where to start looking. I guess you've got the border pretty well blocked?"

"We don't have enough men stationed in the country between the Rio Grande and the Gila to close the border completely," Dinwoodie said, frowning. "And it's even worse between here and the Pecos. East of the Pecos we don't have anything."

While the major talked, Longarm had lighted a fresh cigar. He looked at the major through a dense cloud of blue smoke as he said, "Then I reckon that's where I oughta start looking."

"It's where I'd start, if I was going out on the kind of

job you are," Dinwoodie agreed. "But I'm afraid I can't give you much in the way of support."

"Why, I ain't asking you for nothing more'n a good horse and the rations I'll need to see me through a spell," Longarm told him. "In my book, there's just one thing wrong with the way the army does things."

"And what's that?"

"You send out too many men to do a little bitty job. They make so much of a fuss getting to where they're going, that whoever you've sent 'em after has gotten clean away by the time they get there," Longarm replied. "Now, I just sorta mosey along quiet-like, all by myself, when I'm after somebody. Chances are I won't spook 'em off before I catch up with 'em, and after that it's them against me."

"I see your point," the army officer agreed. "Well, I wish you luck, Marshal Long. Now, suppose I go with you to the sutler's and the stables. I'll save you some money by being with you at the sutler's and I'll see that you get the best horse we've got in the stables."

"I'd appreciate it, Major," Longarm said. "And maybe you can save me some time at both places. I got a passel of miles to cover, and the sooner I set out, the better."

Because he was now in the heart of Apache country, Longarm had not planned to light a fire when he stopped for the night, even if there'd been any vegetation he could have used for fuel. He'd started scanning the rough, barren landscape two hours before sunset, looking for the telltale trace of greenery that would indicate the location of a spring or water hole, but so far he'd seen nothing that might indicate even a single drop of moisture.

Reining in, he twisted in the saddle and fished in his saddlebag until his fingers encountered the map that he'd gotten from Major Dinwoodie when he'd started from Fort Bliss three days earlier. This was the first time during the long trip that he'd felt the need to look at the map. Although the trail he'd set out to follow was dim at best, and vanished for several miles at a stretch in some places, there'd been enough signs of it to keep him from losing it.

Now, with the low sun making it necessary for him to follow the shadow he and the army remount nag cast on the almost-invisible signs of the trail ahead, Longarm was barely able to spot enough traces of its use to be sure he was heading for his chosen destination. So he consulted the map to be sure.

"Old son," he told himself, speaking aloud just to break the desert's silence as he flicked a match into flame and lighted a fresh cigar, "looks like you might as well settle for making a dry camp tonight. Someplace that ain't too far ahead you're bound to find a crack in this damn dry dirt that you can shelter in. But you better keep looking real hard, because it's getting too dark to see."

Only a thin strip of fading pink remained of daylight when Longarm saw a dark sinuous line breaking the yellow earth ahead. He poked the flanks of his tiring mount with his booted heels to speed it up. When his first touch had no effect, Longarm put a bit more force into a second prod and the animal began to move faster. By the time he'd reached the broken line in the earth, he had already formed an idea of what he might find. When he reined in at the edge of the jagged crack that broke the soil, he found that his expectation was fulfilled. The welcome glint of slowly moving water met his eyes.

"Looks like you lucked out this time," Longarm muttered as he looked up from the creek and turned his attention to the thin fissure that held its bed.

Downstream, perhaps a quarter of a mile, the fissure spread into the shallow gap of a miniature canyon. Reining the horse along the edge of the small crevasse, Longarm could see where the creek widened several hundred yards ahead. When he reached the point where the streambed widened and ran shallow in a short, flat-bottomed canyon, there was still enough light for him to see three or four dark blotches, all that remained of some old campfires.

Deciding that he'd find no better place to stop for the night, Longarm scanned the surrounding landscape with a few quick flicks of his eyes, but there was nothing visible in any direction except more sandy soil and the steadily darkening sky. Dismounting, he went directly to the edge of the little trickling creek and bent to scoop up water in his cupped hand. He tasted it and found it sweet, with no alkalai taint, then scooped up another palmful and drank.

His thirst satisfied, Longarm went back to the horse, pulled the tether rope and picket pin from the saddle string that held them, and stomped the pin into the hard soil near enough to the creek for the animal to reach the water. He untied the horse's nose bag from the cantle strap that held it in place and fastened on the horse's muzzle. The horse began munching, and Longarm left it to eat while he loosened the strap of his saddle scabbard and carried the Winchester a few steps upstream until he found a reasonably flat spot a few yards from the stream bank.

Laying the Winchester on the ground to mark the place he'd chosen, Longarm returned to the horse and took off his saddle. He dropped the saddle a few feet away from the animal and returned to the horse long enough to remove the nose bag so the animal could drink. Then he carried his saddle, saddlebags, and bedroll upstream to the place marked by his rifle. There he spread the blanket and pad, untied his bedroll, and opened it out on the saddle blanket.

Hunkering down on the blanket, Longarm groped in his saddlebags until his fingers encountered his necessary bag. He pulled out the oilskin pouch that held his backup rations and munched a mouthful of dried corn to mush before biting off a chunk of jerky and chewing it with the corn until both were soft enough to swallow. A second double-mouthful and another swallow of water finished his supper.

Unbuckling his gun belt, Longarm laid it beside the saddle, stretched out with his head on the skirt's soft leather, and within a few minutes was asleep.

A short, sharp whinny from the remount horse brought Longarm from a sound sleep. He sat up, instantly alert. The animal whinnied a second time. When his ears caught the faint thin sound of a distant horse whinnying in reply, Longarm lifted his rifle from the ground before stretching flat on his belly on the bedroll again. He tried to pierce the veil of night with his eyes, but the darkness of the desert was complete.

There was no moon, no starshine, and even Longarm's night-adjusted eyes could not pierce the blackness. Glancing up, he saw no stars, only the total black gloom of a cloud-covered sky.

He lay without moving and after a moment faint noises, too distant to mean anything, reached his ears. The noises grew a bit louder and Longarm's horse whinnied once more. Again the distant nicker of a second horse responded, but it was louder now. Then faint, unidentifiable sounds began drifting to him, carried by the fitful breeze.

In a moment or two Longarm could not only identify the sounds as horses' hooves grating on the hard-baked soil, but could make out voices. Then he caught a word or two, a man's voice: "...*no estoy errado! Era un caballo!*"

A second voice responded, "*Pues, caballo desierto. Hay algunos aqui.*"

"*Tal vez,*" the first speaker said, "*tambien hay aqui los soldados gringos.*"

"*Que tonteria!*" the second replied.

Longarm understood most of what had been said by the men who were approaching, enough to allow him to guess the rest. He decided to deal himself in before they got too close.

"*Alto!*" he called, sure that at least they'd understand his command. "'*Stoy*—"

Cutting off the remainder of what Longarm had intended to say, a rifle shot broke the still night air. The spurt of yellow muzzle blast that accompanied the shot had been bright enough and near enough to impress itself on his night-sensitive eyes. He batted his eyelids quickly to clear them of the effects of the sudden unexpected light, and as he blinked he heard the thud of fast-fading hoofbeats as the men who'd been approaching turned their horses and spurred them in retreat.

Though Longarm's night vision returned quickly, there was nothing except darkness in front of him, darkness and the steadily diminishing thuds of hoofbeats hanging in the night air. As such noises do in the night, the thuds faded quickly. Though Longarm strained his eyes to pierce the gloom, he saw nothing, and soon the hoofbeats became soft, barely audible pats that seemed to reach his ears from all directions at the same time, and shortly after that the night air held only silence.

Longarm had spent too many years in his chosen trade to fall into the tempting trap of trying to follow the horsemen in the darkness. He knew that night noise could be a two-edged sword, giving away the location of both the pursued and the pursuer. He went back to his bedroll, put aside the temptation to light a cigar, and stretched out. Though he lay awake for some time, he heard no more sounds coming through the black night. After he'd maintained his vigil for what he considered enough time to allow the night riders to return if they intended to, he went back to sleep.

False dawn showed as a grey tinge along the line of the horizon in the east when Longarm woke up. Though the sky held a thin, curving, half-bright glow, the sun was not yet high enough for its rays to touch the earth. Longarm did not get up; he was familiar with the phenomenon and remained comfortably in his bedroll. He lighted a morning cigar and enjoyed it in leisurely puffs while he waited for the first rays of the rising sun to touch the earth and usher in the real dawn.

Pink tinged the sky in the true dawn before Longarm had smoked his stogie to the butt. He rolled out of his blankets now and shoved his feet into his boots. Then he made short work of giving the horse a bagful of grain, and while the animal munched, Longarm rolled his blankets into their usual neat, tight packet and secured them with his saddle strings. He let the horse drink again, saddled it, and mounted. Then he set out to find the trail of the night-riding strangers who'd shot at him the night before.

Their trail was not hard to pick up, for the night riders had spurred away at a gallop following Longarm's call. He spotted the hoofprints of one of the horses almost at once when he'd reached the spot where he'd encountered them the evening before.

Leading away from the place where the night riders had turned back, half-moon-shaped dents of their horses' shod hooves were cut deeply into the hard desert soil, and their galloping pace had sent small clumps of crusted dirt flying. The low-slanting rays of the rising sun created dark shadows beside each clump, and Longarm found that he could keep his horse at a brisk walk without losing the trail.

"Either them horses were damn big critters, or they were toting more of a load than men on their backs, old son," Longarm told himself as he rode. "If they were carrying loads, there sure must've been something about 'em those men didn't want nobody to see. If they hadn't been trying to hide it, they wouldn't've wheeled and run the way they did."

He kept to the trail across the arid desert soil while the sun rose higher and began to discharge its daily load of heat. He'd gotten three or four miles from the place where he'd passed the night, the trail leading him roughly parallel to the little trickle of the stream, when the hoofprints veered abruptly. They led him across the trickling creek and almost at right angles to it. Now the trail was plainer, for more than one set of hooves had churned its surface.

Reining in, Longarm took out a cheroot and lighted it, then hooked his knee around the saddle horn and studied the broken ground that stretched away in front of him. That the trail was well used had been obvious at first glance. Now the low-slanting sun made his observation easy, even though he did not dismount for a really close examination.

There was no need to dismount, for the evidence of

the hoofprints indicated there had been dozens of horses, more than likely scores of them, ridden along the trace. From the evidence of the footprints, traffic over the trail was about evenly divided as to numbers, but the heavily loaded horses were moving south. The depth to which the hoofprints had sunk in the hard-baked soil showed that quite clearly.

"There's two things about these damn tracks that don't jibe, old son," Longarm muttered under his breath.

He stood up in his stirrups to gain a bit more height as he studied the terrain ahead. He found it featureless, though in the distance there was a formation of mesas and buttes, and beyond them the ground rose swiftly in an isolated outcrop of the mountains that broke the ultimate horizon.

Settling back into his saddle, he resumed his study of the hoofprints. Shaking his head, he muttered under his breath, "This ain't no redskin trail. Them horses are all shod. That means it's got to be a smuggling trail, but the damn thing's all backwards. The prints heading toward Mexico were made by loaded horses, and there ain't a thing in this part of the world that ain't easier to find on the other side of the border and cheaper than it is over here. But whatever it is, you better let the Apaches wait a little spell and find out about it."

Chapter 6

Longarm continued to study the tracks for a few moments, then wheeled his horse and started following the trail of hoofprints to the north. The prints ran string-straight toward the spot where the mesas and buttes jutted above the sand. Longarm quickly realized that he'd forgotten how deceptive the desert air could be with its constant heat haze, which began forming in midmorning and reached its peak in the late afternoon. Yesterday afternoon, when he'd first noticed the rock formation, he'd viewed it through the heat haze, and the air's constant shimmer had caused the rock outcrop to seem closer than it actually was.

He rode for more than an hour before reaching his destination. First he passed through a scatter of sage that rose from the rippled sand dunes, then he found it necessary to circle an expanse of jagged humps of chalky limestone rising above the sand. By now he was close enough to realize that what he'd taken to be a rock outcrop was in reality the beginning of a major upthrust of the sandstone that underlay the shifting surface of the desert.

He followed the dim trail through a scattering of raw-faced limestone boulders. Between the boulders yucca grew, the metallic green of their topping spikes interspersed with tiny bell-like blossoms. Joshua trees with crazily twisted limbs thrust up here and there between the yuccas, and less frequently a growth of ocotilla cactus sprawled, the thick spiky shoots of the plants' grey-green limbs looking like saws with double-toothed edges.

Suddenly the dry desert soil sloped sharply downward, a steep, sparsely vegetated terrace broken by the unexpected rise of a sheer-faced limestone outcrop. Rearing back in his saddle, Longarm fought the reins as his remount horse hunkered down on its haunches and stiffened its forelegs to keep itself from somersaulting down the precipitous slant.

If there had been any doubt in his mind that he was still on the trail of the horsemen he was following, it was dispelled now. In the occasional landscape-searching glances he allowed himself during the moments his horse fought the steep slope, Longarm saw the freshly plowed streaks where they had fought the slope, just as he was doing.

At last he reached the bottom of the drop. He reined in the panting horse and looked around, then his jaw dropped. He was looking at the last thing he'd expected to see in such an expanse of generally level desert sand. The striated face of what he'd thought to be merely a small limestone outcrop stretched away from him for a half mile. Weathered by centuries of eroding blasts of windblown sand, the face of the massive bluff had been sculpted into columns and curves that no stone carver could imagine or duplicate.

There was only one spot where the asymetric striations were interrupted. At the base of the bluff, not quite in its center, the jagged yawning face of the limestone bluff was broken by a gaping arc, black and mysteriously inviting. The hoofprints that Longarm had been following led along the foot of the sheer limestone wall and disappeared into the black gap.

"Damned if you ain't found yourself a cave, old son," Longarm said.

His voice and the panting of his horse were the only sounds that broke the still desert air. He slipped a cigar from his vest pocket and lighted it without taking his eyes off the dark arch that broke the bluff's face. Through the wreath of blue-grey cigar smoke that hung around Longarm's face before it was swirled up by the rising heated air, he studied the opening and the lines of hoofprints that disappeared into the cave.

"Well, now," he went on, "looks like there's quite a few folks that have business in that cave. It might just be interesting to go in and see what it is that's bringing 'em to a lonesome place like this."

Toeing his mount ahead, Longarm angled toward the black gap. As he drew closer he saw that there'd be no need to dismount outside; the entrance to the cave was what seemed to be an impossibly big archway, the top of its rim dozens of feet above his head. His horse entered the opening without hesitation, and now its feet thunked gratingly on stone instead of their noise being swallowed by softer earth. Then after it had gone a few steps farther and reached the zone where the grey light from the opening gave way to total blackness, it balked and snorted, then stopped.

Longarm prodded the animal's flank with his boot tip, but the horse took only three or four steps before it stopped once more, unwilling to penetrate the zone where the light from the entrance faded and gave way to impenetrable blackness. Longarm urged it forward by prodding with the toe of his boot, but the animal only tossed its head and snorted shrilly while standing obstinately still.

Gazing from side to side, Longarm saw nothing but darkness. He could form no idea of the size of the chamber he'd entered. On both sides as well as above and ahead of him there was nothing but yawning blackness, and he wondered what the darkness held to explain the odor that was now reaching his nostrils. He looked back at the yellow arch through which he'd entered. It glowed bright yellow with the sunshine outside, but the light coming through it was confined to a streak of brightness that after a few dozen feet began merging with the interior's darkness and offered no clue as to the width of the cavern.

"Looks like you might've bit off a chunk that's a mite too big for you to chew and swallow down, old son," he said in a half whisper. In spite of himself, Longarm was a bit awed by the size of the cavern he'd stumbled onto. "But all of those tracks outside show horses coming in here and going out. One thing's sure as God made little green apples: If the ones that left them tracks were anyplace close, you'd know it by now. And if somebody else is smart enough to figure out how to go on farther into this place, you sure oughta be, too."

As was his habit when faced with a problem requiring thought to solve, Longarm fingered a cigar out of his vest pocket. He clamped the long thin stogie between his teeth and fingered a match from his vest pocket. Flicking his thumbnail across the match head, he brought the flaming sliver up to light his cigar, and was bending forward to light the stogie when a voice from the darkness at one side of him broke the cave's stillness.

"Levantese las manos o matase!" the speaker said sharply.

Longarm obeyed in spite of his surprise that it was a woman who'd commanded him to raise his hands or be killed. He'd faced more than enough gun-wielding women during his long career as a lawman to recognize the fixed purpose conveyed by the voice of the speaker. Her tone left no doubt in his mind that she would carry out her threat and put a bullet into him if he hesitated or refused to obey her. He let the lighted match fall and raised his hands above his head.

"Bueno," she said. *"Tienes español, sí?"*

Again experience dictated Longarm's response. "I savvy just about enough to understand what you told me to do," he replied. "But I don't talk it good enough to follow much more'n that."

"Then I will speak English," she said.

Longarm's keen ears caught the faint rustle of cloth moving, and in a moment the woman's voice came from behind him. "You will get down from your horse. Then you will lead it and walk straight to the front of you."

"How in tunket do you expect me to do that?" Longarm asked. "I can't see where I'm going in the dark."

"You will have light *prontito*," she replied. *"Pues,* do as I say."

As Longarm swung out of his saddle, the woman whistled loudly, a shrill note that rang echoing through the darkened cavern, quavered like the call of some large bird, and ended on another high piercing note. Before Longarm had taken three steps, leading his horse by its reins, he saw the glow of a lantern forming an amber streak of light from the stone floor of the cavern to its dome, thirty feet or more above his head.

Growing brighter minute by minute, the glow spread across the top of the vast underground chamber, down its curved walls and along its stone floor. Only then did Longarm realize the vastness of the cave he'd entered. From the spot where he was at the moment, near the center of the irregularly circled chamber through which he was moving with deliberate slowness, fifty or sixty feet still separated him from the vertical line of lantern glow.

On his right the wall was even more distant, and the left half of the chamber was still veiled in gloom. When he turned his head in that direction to risk a quick backward glance, he got a vague glimpse of the moving figure of the woman who'd taken him by surprise. The distance between them was too great and the darkness in that direction still too deep for him to see her clearly. The darkness obscured her face and he could glimpse her only as a moving form in the murky gloom, but during the few seconds he risked looking toward her, he also saw that she had not been bluffing.

She carried a rifle, holding it slanted across her body as a skilled marksman will, in the position that would allow her to shoulder the gun and shoot in less time than he'd need to draw his Colt. She was moving behind him, following at the slow steady pace he'd set in his forward movement.

During the few moments required to make his quick observations, Longarm had kept moving steadily ahead. The strange odor that he'd noticed before was stronger

64

now. His progress was accompanied by the metallic clanking of his horse's shod feet, echoing and doubling the thunk of his own boot soles. His eyes grew accustomed to the glowing light ahead as he made his slow progress, and when he finally reached the far end of the huge chamber and came to the end of the wall which had shielded the light bearer, he could see clearly once more.

Longarm had taken only a step beyond the wall's end when the woman raised her voice again. "Stop now! Do not make a move or I will shoot you!"

As he came to a halt, Longarm had turned his head involuntarily, looking for the source of the light that broke the darkness of the vast chamber through which he'd entered the underground formation. Before turning his head to the front again, he got a glimpse of a small man holding an old-fashioned bulbous railroad lantern, a tin globe with a spout at its top, from which a lighted cotton wick protruded. The muzzle of the woman's rifle prodded him in the back and he froze in place, his arms at his sides, being very careful not to move a muscle.

"Enciende el farol," she said. *"Y tome el fusil, también la pistola. Y despues, vete al jefe y digale ventá 'ca. Andale, hijo!"*

Longarm had carried out enough assignments in Mexico and along the border to understand Spanish reasonably well. He was prepared when the small man placed the lantern on the floor and came to his side. At close range, he saw with some surprise that the small man was actually a youth, perhaps no older than his early teens. He wore the loosely fitted cotton jacket and trousers common to the border dwellers, and his bare feet were encased in flat-soled huaraches.

In spite of his youth, the lad showed a caution that

could have come only from experience. He kept his eyes fixed on Longarm's hands rather than his face, and stopped while still out of easy grasp. Pointing to the rifle, he extended his arm and held it with the palm of his hand turned up, until Longarm placed the rifle stock on his palm.

Still keeping his eyes fixed on Longarm, the youth took a step backward and laid the rifle down, then stepped up and indicated with a gesture that he wanted Longarm to turn around. Under the muzzle of the woman's rifle, Longarm had no choice. He made a half turn, and the lad darted forward to pull the Colt from its holster and stepped back as quickly as he'd moved up. Still holding the Colt, he turned and raised his eyebrows at the girl carrying the rifle.

"*Retenese ahorita,*" she replied in response to his unspoken question. "*Pero tomese el fusil y aconteceme al jefe.*"

"*Y el caballo?*" he asked.

"*Posteriormente,*" the woman said with a shrug. "*Vaminos ahorita.*" She turned her full attention to Longarm again and went on. "We will go now. Walk slowly and carefully. I do not wish to shoot such a big handsome man, but I will if you do not do what I have told you."

"I figure if you'd wanted to shoot me, you'd've done it by now," Longarm told her. "Far as I can tell now, I ain't got no reason to bother you, even if you do wave that rifle around pretty free."

When his attempt at a casual remark had no effect on the girl except for her to swing her rifle to indicate that he was to follow the youth, Longarm stepped away from his horse. The youth had picked up the lamp and the rifle and started down the dark corridor that branched off the huge chamber, and Longarm followed him, always aware of the woman and her rifle at his back.

Although the gently curving corridor was large, it did not share the vastness of the chamber by which Longarm had entered the underground world. They'd taken only a few steps before the solid stone floor grew rough and striated with slanting veins of the same light, creamy stone that formed its walls and its ceiling, which arced gently ten or a dozen feet above their heads.

Here the light was more effective, and the cream-white walls of the tunnellike corridor reflected and amplified its flame. The smell had increased in intensity as well. Before they'd taken a dozen steps Longarm was aware that the shushing scrape of the youth's huaraches and the thud of his boot heels were the only noises he heard. He risked turning for a quick glance at the woman and saw that she was barefoot. She held the rifle across her chest, ready to bring it to her shoulder, and her eyes were fixed on him. Longarm turned his eyes back toward the lad, and kept moving at the same steady pace that the light carrier was setting.

They'd walked for perhaps ten minutes when the corridor began to grow brighter and its curving more pronounced. Then abruptly the corridor ended in a room as big as the vast chamber by which Longarm had entered. This huge vaulted opening was not dark, however. Miners' lamps of the same kind as the one carried by the youth burned at intervals on the floor, and a few had been placed in rock outcrops that formed small, natural shelves on the walls.

Longarm paid little attention to such details, however. His attention was drawn at once to a dozen or so men, clad in the same pajamalike garb worn by the youth, who were busy at the far end of the chamber filling small bags from a heap of what seemed to be sand, which was piled on the floor. As Longarm watched, one of the men detached himself from the workers and started toward them.

Even before the man had taken a half-dozen steps, Longarm felt a surge of relief. The approaching man shook his head as though to clear it, then broke into a run.

"Longarm!" he called. "You're the last man on earth I expected to see! What the devil are you doing here and how did you find me?"

By this time his running gait had brought him close enough for Longarm to reply without having to raise his voice. He said casually, hiding his own surprise, "Well, now, that's a funny thing. If I'd known you were in this place, your lady friend wouldn't've had to bring me here with a gun stuck in my tailbone. How the hell are you, Gato?"

They were shaking hands before Longarm asked his question. El Gato, Longarm's companion in several close calls with the rurales and other minions of the corrupt Diaz government that ruled Mexico with iron-shod cruelty, was laughing too heartily to reply at once. When his ringing laughter ended he turned to the young woman who'd captured Longarm and said, *"Ponte abajo su fusil, Graciada. Es un amigo mio, este hombre. No recuerdo que he dicho de Longarm?"*

"Sí, Gato, pero no conozco—" she began, but El Gato waved her to silence and turned back to Longarm.

"Seriously, what are you doing here, Longarm?" he asked. "I didn't know that anybody knew about this place except a few of my friends and myself."

"I didn't," Longarm told him. "This young lady

brought me here, after I stumbled into your cave while I was chasing after a couple of hombres that tried to cut me down out on the damn desert. I didn't even know there was a cave like this anyplace around these parts."

"Few people do," El Gato explained. "Only the Apaches, and they have religious beliefs that keep them from talking about it, or even coming near it. They will not even come here to pick up the gunpowder I sell them. I must have my men deliver it to them at their village in Mexico. It is a difficult matter, of course. The border is three days' ride away."

Before El Gato had finished his explanation, a frown had grown on Longarm's face. His voice was sober when he asked, "You mean you're selling powder to Geronimo and his dirty killers?"

"Of course. Why not? They live in Mexico now, you know. Besides, they pay well, and Madero has no money to support my work here."

"Well, I hate to tell you this, El Gato," Longarm said soberly, making no effort to hide the regret in his voice, "but if you're on Geronimo's side, I ain't got no choice. I got to arrest you, right here and now."

Chapter 7

"You joke, do you not, amigo?" El Gato asked. The tone of his voice told Longarm that he did not consider it a joking matter.

Longarm shook his head. "You know better'n that, Gato. If you're the one that's been keeping Geronimo and his Apaches in gunpowder that he uses when he raids on our side of the border, I got to put a stop to it, even if it means—"

El Gato broke in, "You forget something, amigo. You are the one who is the captive, not me. Your holster is empty, and I see your Colt in Felipe's belt. He and Graciada have rifles, and I suspect they've taken yours, as well. You are alone, and I have only to raise my voice to call to the men you see working over there. Now tell me this, Longarm. Just how do you plan to arrest me?"

"I got to admit, I ain't worked that out yet," Longarm replied. "But you and me've known each other a good spell. You've never seen me back away from any job I set my hand to."

"This is true," El Gato admitted. "But you have not heard my full story yet. Listen to me for a moment, for the sake of our old friendship!"

"You're asking can we have a truce?" Longarm asked.

"Why not?" El Gato shrugged. "Surely after we've fought side by side against Diaz and his rurales we can trust each other and talk as friends for an hour or two."

"I don't reckon talking's going to change much," Longarm answered slowly. "But if you want to give it a try, I'm agreeable."

"Bueno," El Gato said, nodding. He turned to Graciada and said, *"Vuelven a la entrada, tu y Felipe. Deja el hombre y su caballo, yo lo cuidare."*

"While you're telling 'em what to do, you might as well get my Colt and Winchester from the boy," Longarm broke in. "I ain't expecting you to hand them over to me till we got our differences settled, but I'd a sight rather have them where I can keep my eye on them."

El Gato turned to Felipe and held out his hand. *"La pistola y el fusil,"* he said. When the youth handed him Longarm's Colt and Winchester, El Gato tucked the pistol into the waistband of his trousers and set the rifle aside. Then he waved Graciada and Felipe away and turned back to Longarm. "Bueno," he said. "Now, let us see whether we can settle any differences between us. Perhaps you will not even feel like arresting me when you hear what I have to say."

"I'll listen to anything and everything you have to tell me," Longarm said as he walked beside El Gato past the group of men who were filling the small canvas sacks with greyish yellow granules. "But first tell me what in hell stinks so bad."

"Bat droppings," El Gato replied. "Guano. The bats

72

roost in this cave in numbers too huge to count. Their droppings are stacked high in the places where they roost. But it is the guano that keeps us here."

"You sure must be doing something special besides keeping that damned Geronimo in gunpowder."

"I do not apologize for what I do, Longarm," El Gato said. He gestured for Longarm to stop, and stepped over to the wall of the cavern to pick up one of the lights that stood near the wall of the big underground chamber. As he rejoined Longarm, he went on. "I sell gunpowder to Geronimo for only one reason: I need all the money I can get to keep my workers fed."

"Maybe you better start out by telling me why in hell you're making gunpowder at all on this side of the Rio Grande," Longarm suggested.

"It is a long story. And we will talk better together if we have a small *copita* at the same time."

They'd passed the area by now where the men were at work, and El Gato was leading Longarm along a narrowing fissured passageway, a dark natural fracture in the limestone with inward-slanting walls that met only a yard or so above their heads. They reached a spot where the fissure joined a second earth fracture that led off it at an angle. As the fissure was narrowing, the light revealed a narrow cot with a bundled heap of blankets on it. A small stool and table stood beside it. Stacks of papers and a bottle of *aguardiente* filled the tabletop.

"My bedroom and office," El Gato explained. He placed the lamp on the table and waved at the stool to indicate that Longarm was to sit down. He moved the bottle of *aguardiente* closer to Longarm and seated himself on the cot. Indicating the bottle, he went on, saying, "It is not your own drink, I know, but it is the best I have to offer."

"Oh, I got a hunch it'll be a while before I taste Tom Moore again," Longarm told him. "But right now my throat's so dry I'd settle for beer or even water."

He tilted the bottle for a satisfying swallow of the fiery Mexican brandy and passed it to El Gato. After drinking, El Gato placed the bottle on the stone floor between them and looked at Longarm. He said, "Much has happened since we talked last."

"I ain't forgot a bit of what we ran into that time," Longarm replied. He took a cigar from his vest pocket and bent to light it from the flame of the lamp. Through a cloud of smoke he said, "Maybe I ought not say anything about it, Gato."

"*Porque no?* I'm sure we both remember it quite well."

"Sure. But I ain't one to remind a man of a favor I've done him. Besides, you've done me a few favors, too."

Both men sat silent for a moment. Their last encounter had been deep in central Mexico. There, a group of crooked rurales who were involved in a plot to overthrow Mexico's legitimate government and put their own man in power were holding El Gato in prison before executing him. Though El Gato had been using one of his many aliases, Longarm had recognized him at once. As much to help his old friendly enemy as to foil the revolutionaries, Longarm had engineered El Gato's escape. Side by side the pair had fought their way to the border, and El Gato had returned to his homeland.

At last El Gato said, "You are quiet because you know I do not belong on this side of the Rio Grande, Longarm. You wonder whether what I do here is bad or good. So, you have a right to know what I am doing, and I have no objection to telling you, for I am not breaking any of your country's laws."

74

"Not that it'd surprise me if you were," Longarm said, smiling to take away any sting his words might seem to have. "Go ahead and tell me about what you're doing in this cave. I know already that you're making gunpowder, but I got to admit I'm sorta curious about why. You can buy all you want to."

"Not in Mexico," El Gato said. "Not with Diaz back in the office of presidente. He is too afraid the Maderistas will overthrow him if they have ammunition for their guns."

"But gunpowder ain't much use anymore," Longarm argued. "Not unless you got a factory that uses it to load into shells."

El Gato smiled. "It has been too long since you were in my country, Longarm. Only the guns the government provides for the army and the rurales use cartridges. We on the side of Madero have few modern rifles that fire metal cartridges. Our men must use chassepot rifles from France and old guns of that sort. And your old enemy Geronimo, his men have few rifles that fire cartridges. They use the same kind of guns our *peóns* do."

"So you set up shop on this side of the border, and smuggle the gunpowder over to your friends," Longarm said. "Now I got to admit, that never would've occurred to me."

"So far it has not occurred to Diaz and his men, either. They have not enough strength yet to begin the revolution, but the day will come when Madero's forces can defeat Diaz and his army."

"And you're saying that you can turn out enough for your friends in a place like this cave?"

"Much easier in this cave than anywhere else I know of. It is here that we find the necessary *salitre*."

"Salitre?" Longarm frowned as he repeated the word.

"In your language, saltpeter," El Gato explained. "Do you not know how easy it is to make gunpowder, amigo?"

"Now that you mention it, I recall a little bit of what I picked up from my friend Theo Bryson. He's maybe the best gunsmith in the world right now, and his shop's in Denver."

"Your own headquarters, of course," El Gato said.

"Let's see if I remember," Longarm went on. "You got to have saltpeter and sulfur and something else. It's—"

"Charcoal," El Gato said quickly. "With only those three simple things, gunpowder can be made anywhere. And there are some things about this cave we are in that you do not know."

"Which ain't much of a surprise, seeing I didn't know it was even here till I stumbled over it today."

"I stumbled into it by accident several years ago, Longarm, when I was running from the rurales and beat them across the border. I could not be sure they would stop there, so I came on. There were no trails then, and by accident I passed the mouth of the cave. It seemed a good place to hide, so I went in. I hid here another time or two, then when I took up my present work, I remembered it."

"It's a big enough cave to hide a man on the run real good," Longarm agreed. "How big is it, anyhow?"

"That I do not know. I have not gone into much of it, but I do know that it is huge, much bigger than you might think. There are tunnels and chambers much larger than the one where you entered. Why, one of

76

them is so big we use it for a corral, and in some of the walls crystals glow like diamonds."

"Sounds like you've been poking around in it quite a lot."

El Gato shook his head. "There are passages I have never even entered. I have only used it as a place to hide, and it is a good place for one such as I am, who needs to disappear when the—well, when it is better to disappear than go to prison. And in some of its chambers bats roost by the thousands."

"What in the hell have bats got to do with anything?" Longarm frowned.

"Wherever bats roost they leave their droppings," El Gato explained. "And while each bat is small, many thousands of them have been roosting here for many years. In the places they favor, the droppings are ten feet or more deep on the cavern floor. When the droppings dry and a tiny bit of potassium is poured on them, they become saltpeter."

"So that's why you've got them fellows in here with you!" Longarm exclaimed. "You've set up shop to make gunpowder!"

"Exactly," El Gato nodded. "Even the smallest stores in the little towns near ranches carry sulfur in their wares, you must know that."

"I forgot until you mentioned it," Longarm admitted. "It's a prime medicine for steers."

"Charcoal, that is easy for us to make. We go to the mountains a few miles west and find dead trees to burn."

"But you still got to have that stuff you named a minute ago, that potassium. Where do you find it?"

"We do not find it, amigo." El Gato reached under the cot he was sitting on and held up a chamber pot.

"We make it each time one of us makes water. A few miles to the north there is a big field of potash. We dissolve a bit in the pot here, and it is enough to treat many pounds of bat droppings."

"Well, I guess I've heard everything now," Longarm said after he'd puffed his cigar silently for a moment. "Here you are running a regular gunpowder factory!" Longarm exclaimed. "And your gunpowder ain't for sale, you smuggle it into Mexico for your friends who're trying to get rid of Diaz!"

"Exactly." El Gato nodded. "We are trying to get all the supplies we will need. If we were to come across the border and try to buy as much as we must have, it would bring on talk. The talk would get back to Diaz, and he would move on us before we are ready."

"Even if it meant he'd have to come across the border into this country to get at you?"

"I did not speak clearly. I did not mean that Diaz would come here. He would begin to arrest my friends in Mexico who support Madero. There are some our movement cannot spare. If they were to be arrested, our plans would be crippled."

"When are you going to spring this scheme of yours, Gato?"

"*Quien sabe?*" El Gato shrugged. "A month, three months, a year, perhaps even more. Money is hard to find in Mexico, mi amigo. That is why I sell a few pounds to the Apaches now and then, as I have already told you. The money we get for it buys our food and the sulfur we need."

"It's them few pounds you sell to Geronimo's Apaches that I ain't going to be able to swallow, Gato," Longarm said soberly. "The way I heard it told, Diaz made 'em swear not to fight your people before he'd let 'em come into Mexico, so now they come over on this side of the border to raid and kill."

"This is as I heard it, too," El Gato agreed.

"And the Apaches are mortal devils. The guns they use might be old ones, but they know how to make good use of 'em, killing folks on this side of the border."

"I like the Apaches as little as you do," El Gato said. "But if I do not sell them gunpowder someone else will."

"I reckon you're right about that," Longarm agreed. "But I still don't feel like I want to—" He broke off as a gunshot sounded from somewhere in the cavern.

El Gato jumped to his feet. "Something is wrong!" he said. "I must go and find out! If it is—" He broke off as another shot reverberated, the sound magnifying and seeming to pulse in the still air of the cave.

"Sounds like to me somebody's jumped your men in that big room," Longarm said.

Now shots were breaking the air almost constantly. Now and then a yell could be heard between the wide-spaced shooting.

"It is at the cave mouth," El Gato told Longarm. "I must go and see what is happening."

"I'll go along, then. Whatever it is, it sure ain't likely to be good news."

"This isn't your fight, Longarm," El Gato pointed out.

"Maybe it ain't as much mine as it is yours, Gato, but we've been helping each other long enough that I ain't about to quit now. You come down to it, we're in the same hole together."

"You'll need your pistol, then," El Gato said. He took the Colt out of his waistband and handed it to

79

Longarm, then went on as he picked up the lantern. "I meant to return it to you before now."

Side by side, with El Gato carrying the flickering light, they hurried back toward the chamber where the powder was being made. The gunfire was sporadic now and the yells more frequent. Only an occasional shot sounded now, with a long interval before the next, but the echoes that followed each shot made it seem that a major battle was taking place.

When Longarm and El Gato reached the cavern where the powder was mixed, they found it deserted. There had been no shots for several minutes, but as they rushed toward the passageway to the outer cavern, a fresh volley of shooting broke out.

"Something's happening down at the cave mouth!" Longarm said to El Gato.

"My men have pushed back the attackers!" El Gato exclaimed. "They are good fighters! If we hurry and give them a little help we can surely drive away our enemies!"

By this time Longarm and El Gato were crossing the big cavern used as the workroom for mixing the powder in its final stages. The lofty room was deserted and the tools of the men who worked in it were lying abandoned. They hurried across the area to the wide corridor and started down it.

A few scattered shots echoed from the stone walls of the passageway, and now they could hear faint shouts. They reached the outer chamber. The men from the powder-mixing room were in two clusters, one group on each side of the lofty arched entrance. At first glance they seemed to be doing nothing but firing an occasional scattered shot in response to the ragged shooting that sounded from outside, but as Longarm watched them while he and El Gato were hugging the wall and circling to reach the entrance, he could see that they were following a very methodical pattern.

One man from each side of the arch stepped up from the group and aimed at the attackers and let off his round. Then he stepped back to take his place in the small groups sheltered at each side of the entry and began reloading his single-shot rifle while another man took his place and fired. The shooting was not heavy, but it was consistent, and seemed to be holding the attackers at bay.

One of the men saw Longarm and El Gato approaching and left the rotating line to hurry up to them. El Gato asked, *"Que pasa ahorita, Ernando? Quien atacaba?"*

"No conozco, Gato," the man replied. *"Tal vez los Indios, tal vez los rurales. Todo lo que se que Graciada fue herida delante."*

Longarm could understand only part of the man's reply, but caught enough to understand that Graciada was in trouble. He asked El Gato, "What'd he say about the girl?"

"She's wounded and trapped outside the cave," El Gato replied. "But he doesn't know who's attacking us. It could be either the rurales or Geronimo's Apaches."

"It don't make much difference who's doing the shooting out there, Gato," Longarm said. He took a step aside to get a clear look at the area beyond the cavern opening, then turned back, saying, "Cover me, Gato. I'll go bring her in."

Chapter 8

Before El Gato could reply, Longarm turned and started for the cave mouth. Hugging the edge of the entrance arch he peered outside. The first thing he saw was a dozen horses tethered on the high level land beyond the sparsely vegetated upslope that led away from the mouth of the cave. They were well beyond the range of gunfire, in the thicker clumps of cactus and ocotilla and yucca and Joshua trees that dotted the sand dunes stretching away from the rise.

After a moment spent examining the cactus clumps, Longarm located Graciada. She was lying prone, pressed down on the baked soil twenty yards from the mouth of the cavern, behind a tall thick cluster of yucca. She was not moving, and for a moment Longarm thought she'd been badly wounded, perhaps even fatally so. Then she moved, trying to peer back over her shoulder at the cave.

Longarm took his hat off and pushed it beyond the edge of the entrance arch to draw the attention of the attackers away from her. A scattering of gunfire rattled and puffs of muzzle blast rose here and there among the widely spaced clusters of cactus that provided the only cover on the slope beyond the cave's black opening. Longarm pulled his hat back quickly. In a moment the shooting stopped. El Gato's voice, coming from Longarm's side, broke the silence that followed the hail of shots.

"There are too many of them out there, amigo," he said. "At least ten or a dozen. I know what you're thinking, but it is not a good idea. You might get to Graciada, but you would never get back, carrying her."

"Maybe," Longarm said, and triggered off a shot of his own. The burst of firing in response to his shot gave Longarm an idea. He turned to El Gato and said, "You wait here a minute and let off a round now and then, just to let 'em know we're still watching. I have to go get something that'll help us."

"Only time will help us! I will bring more men up here and they can cover us when—"

Longarm broke in to say, "Listen to me, Gato! I have the medicine we need to cure them fellows. Now just let off a shot or two, keep 'em pinned down while I'm gone. Then we'll get Graciada back in two shakes of a lamb's tail."

Before El Gato could reply, Longarm was gone, his booted feet clattering on the cavern's limestone floor. He stopped when he reached the big room where the powder-making crew worked. The lights by which they worked had been left behind when the men rushed to defend their hideout, and Longarm had to stop and blink for a moment before he could see clearly.

Even then it was his nose rather than his eyes which led him to the horses. He followed the odor of manure to the rough arch leading to the stable cavern. His horse

84

had not yet been unsaddled. He dug into the bag in which he'd put Theo Bryson's automatic gun and managed to fit the stock and barrel together while he was running back to the entrance.

"Here," he told El Gato as he handed him the odd, L-shaped weapon. "Soon as I get started back with the girl, you spray the bushes where the rurales are holed up. Just keep the muzzle sorta high so you won't hit us by mistake."

"What is this you have given me?" El Gato asked. His voice revealed his perplexity.

"It's a rapid-fire gun," Longarm replied. He put his finger on the action just above the trigger. "That's the trigger right there. Don't hold it down longer'n a second or two, and remember that the muzzle's going to want to pull up away from you when you start shooting."

While he and El Gato were talking, the gunfire outside had slackened, but a new burst of shots came from the cavern's besiegers when Longarm emerged at a run and started toward the yucca that sheltered Graciada.

On both sides and in front of him bullets raised small geysers of sand from the soil's baked surface, but the men scattered outside the cave had not been expecting a rescue effort. Longarm reached Graciada's hiding place unharmed and dropped to the ground beside her.

"How bad you hurt?" he asked.

"A small wound, but it is in my foot. I cannot walk or run," she replied.

"Then it looks like I got to carry you," he said.

"But if you carry me you cannot move fast or dodge!" she objected.

"Never mind that. If it works out like I got planned, we won't need to."

"No! Wait until El Gato sends men out to help!"

85

"He ain't going to send nobody out. I told him I'd get you back to the cave if he'd cover us while we get up that slope to the opening."

"How can he do that by himself?"

"Just hang on to me and you'll see quick enough. Get ready, now. I'm going to grab you and boost you up, and you jump as best you can. Then take hold of my shirt or whatever's handiest and don't let go till we're safe inside the cave."

Longarm hunkered down and closed his big hands around Graciada's waist. He lifted her effortlessly and tossed her over his shoulder, then rose and turned in one swift move and began running toward the cave's entrance.

Shots began cracking from behind them as soon as Longarm rose and started running. Then, before he'd taken three giant strides, the musical chatter of Theo's rapid-fire weapon overrode the random firing from the men on the slope.

El Gato was heeding Longarm's instructions. He fired short bursts of no more than six or eight shots, and the angry yells and silent guns from the area occupied by the attackers testified eloquently to their surprise at the machine gun's unaccustomed chatter.

Longarm was halfway to the cave's mouth before the men hidden in the yucca and cacti began shooting again. When they did recover and begin squeezing off aimed shots, their gunfire came too late and was too slow and scattered. Longarm had counted on them being surprised, but had not realized that the surprise factor would be so important. He was up the slope and carrying Graciada into the dark yawning mouth of the cavern before the attackers realized that they no longer had a target and stopped shooting.

"This is one hell of a fine gun, amigo!" El Gato said when Longarm stopped beside him inside the cave. On both sides of the great arched entrance to the cavern the workers gathered in small groups, talking excitedly, some of them pointing at the gun which El Gato still held. "Where can I get one like it?"

"I'm afraid you can't," Longarm replied. "But I'll tell you more about it later. Right now, get some of these fellows to take Graciada back deeper in the cave and fix up her foot. Then you hustle on back here and stand right where you are now with the gun."

"*De seguro, amigo,*" El Gato replied.

He hurried away and returned within little more than a minute, two of the powder makers with him. He gave them orders in a burst of staccato Spanish, and they lifted Graciada and carried her carefully away. Then El Gato turned back to Longarm.

"What foolishness do you plan next?" he asked.

"I'm going out there with a flag of truce and see if I can talk some sense into them fellows," Longarm told him. "I never did get a good look at any of 'em, but from the sound of the guns they were using, I'll bet a silver dollar to a plugged nickel they ain't Indians."

"They are rurales," El Gato said. "I got a good look at two or three of them while they were moving around. But talking to them will be time wasted."

"Just the same, I got to do it. This ain't Mexico, Gato. Them fellows is on the American side of the border now, and once they get in the habit of coming over here any time they feel like it, you and your folks are going to be in real trouble."

"You speak the truth," El Gato agreed. "But if you wish to try to persuade them to leave, I will not object. I will even go with you, if you wish, since you have no Spanish."

"You ain't going out there, Gato! Them murdering rurales are likely to shoot you on sight!"

"There is truth in what you say," El Gato agreed. "Do what you choose, then."

Longarm took off his hat and began waving it up and down at the edge of the arched entry. He signaled for several moments before one of the men outside responded.

"Que tal?" the rurale called.

Longarm turned to El Gato and said, "I guess you better start the talking. Find out first if there's any of 'em that know English."

El Gato nodded, then yelled out, *"Queremos hablar, pero hablamos en inglés! Y no tiren! Es agradable?"*

A long minute ticked past before the reply came, then the rurale shouted, *"Es agradable.* We weel espeak the *inglés* and we weel not eshoot first! *Vete ahorita!"*

El Gato shook his head. "You surprise me, Longarm. How did you know they'd agree?"

"Just a hunch I had. I'll go see what I can do."

"Drop flat if there's trouble," El Gato advised him. "I'll be ready to shoot if they try any tricks."

His eyes still on the slope, Longarm nodded. Then he left the protection of the cavern mouth and started walking slowly toward the patchy cover growth. He'd taken only a few steps before a man halfway up the slope stepped from behind a thick clump of ocotilla and began walking to meet him. He kept his eyes as steadily on Longarm as Longarm did on him. The man wore the short, gold-embroidered charro jacket, bottom-flared trousers, and peak-creased sombrero that had through the years become almost an obligatory uniform for the rurales.

As Longarm advanced he kept his eyes busy. At closer range he could spot the cover chosen by several of the rurales, for in clumps of the tall, spindly yucca and behind the taller, thicker-growing ocotilla he could see glints of metal. Halfway down the gentle slope he was descending, the approaching rurale stopped. Longarm kept advancing until only a dozen feet separated the two, then he stopped as well.

Although Longarm was well aware by technicality he was no longer a deputy U.S. marshal, he'd already decided that he'd cling to the title. As he came to a halt he said, "My name's Long. Deputy United States marshal outa the Denver office."

"Florentino Salazar. *Fuerza de Rurales,* Romero de la República de Mexico," the other man replied.

"I guess you men know this ain't Mexican territory," Longarm said calmly. "You're in the United States now, New Mexico Territory, and you got no authority here. Now, I'll give you ten minutes to mount up and ride back across the border."

"We were not aware we had crossed the border," the rurale replied. His English was impeccable. "We were pursuing a fugitive and one of us saw him take shelter in that cave behind you."

"It's funny none of us in the cave saw him come in," Longarm told the rurale. "And it's funny you shot that little lady that I took in the cave a few minutes ago, and began shooting at me when I came out to get her."

"We have made the mistake," Salazar said. His voice held a faintly mocking tone. "In the distance when we first saw her we took her for the fugitive we were trying to overtake. For this and for any other mistakes we might have made in our zeal to enforce the law, we offer an apology."

"Maybe you better tell me who's in charge of that outfit of yours," Longarm said. His anger at the impossible situation in which he found himself was growing by the minute, but he could think of nothing which would enable him to change it.

"I am, señor. My rank is lieutenant, and I have given you my name."

"So you did," Longarm said soberly. "Now, Lieutenant, I'll ask you to get your men together and ride back to your own country before you make any more fool mistakes like you just done."

"We will start at once, of course," Salazar replied. "But I hope that if any problem has arisen from our unfortunate error, you will be prepared to overlook it, as I am sure my *comandante* will when I report to him."

"I guess all we can do is wait and see, ain't it?" Longarm told the rurale. "Anyway, I ain't got anything else to say, Lieutenant. Except that I'll be standing right here watching while you and your outfit rides off."

Salazar had turned away before Longarm finished speaking. Though Longarm knew that the rurale's gesture was an act of calculated rudeness, intended to express contempt for the United States and all its lawmen, he did not challenge the man. He stood watching while the rurale began walking stiffly back to the area where his men were holed up.

Halfway up the slope, Salazar shouted a command, and for the next few minutes it seemed to Longarm that every ocotilla clump and every sprawling stand of yucca had been concealing a rurale. They fell in behind Salazar as he stalked stiff-legged up to the crest, most of them turning now and then to glance back at Longarm, who stood his ground while he watched them disappear over the top of the rise.

When Longarm heard the distant whinnying of horses and the occasional shout of one of the rurales, he started up the slope himself. The rurales were riding away as he reached its crest. They did not maintain a formation, but scattered and straggled in an untidy group, heading more west than south, obviously striking out for the common border shared by Mexico, Texas, and New Mexico Territory. Longarm watched the retreating rurales until a dip in the prairie hid them from sight, then he returned to the mouth of the cave.

"They are gone," El Gato said as Longarm came up. "But do not make any mistake, amigo, they will be back."

"Sure they will," Longarm agreed. "And that Salazar fellow who was in charge of 'em was just daring me to call him a liar when he spun me a yarn about them chasing after some man they wanted. Except he stretched things a little bit far when he said they'd been chasing him from the other side of the border."

"It would have been a very long chase," El Gato said, grinning. "We travel three days each way when we deliver a load of powder across the border."

"Anyway, the rurales ain't likely to be back for a spell," Longarm went on. "So you and your bunch can get back to work."

"And you, amigo? What plans have you?"

"Well, I'm sorta up a stump right now," Longarm confessed. "I found out what I was sent after, to find out where Geronimo and his outfit have been getting their ammunition. Now I got to tell 'em I found out."

"Then the United States Army will be sent here to

our cave, and there will be a great deal of unpleasant-ness," El Gato said. "Am I not right?"

"Oh, you hit it square, Gato. Soon as the Indian Bureau folks can get the army started moving, the soldiers will be here to close your factory down."

"How long do you think it will take them to begin moving?" El Gato frowned.

"That's anybody's guess. From what I picked up while I was at Fort Bliss, this outfit General Crook's putting together to go after Geronimo won't be ready to start for maybe a month."

"In a month we can make several hundred pounds of powder," El Gato said. "If they do not start at once, we will have time to deliver all the powder we have made since our last trip, and then we can come back here and work at making more, until they force us to leave. They will come with the army, as soon as they get your report."

"And you know I got to make one, Gato," Longarm said. "We've been friends a long time, and I hate like sin to put you outa business. But I ain't got no choice."

"This I understand," El Gato agreed. "You must do your duty, just as I do mine."

"How long will it take you to move out the powder you got on hand, Gato?"

"We can start tomorrow, and be back in a week, per-haps a day less if we push our mules."

"Well, I tell you what," Longarm said. "You get ready to go fast as you can, and hurry on back. It'll be a while before the Indian Bureau and the army can start pulling together. You might as well keep working till they get here."

"But what about the cave? If I use all my men, there

will be no one here to watch our equipment. If the rurales should return, they would—"

"Now you just go ahead and get that powder deliv-
ered," Longarm said. "I can't move on or go back to
Denver till I send my report in and get word from my
new boss in the Indian Bureau whether or not my job's
done. This is as good a place for me to stay as any, and
if them rurales come back while you're away, I'd sure
like to be around here to make 'em feel unwelcome."

Chapter 9

"It sure is quiet in here, with El Gato and everybody else but you and me gone," Longarm remarked to Graciada as they sat at the ancient scarred table in El Gato's chamber.

On the table the wavering light of one of the globe-like work lamps cast its yellow glow over the small room. The empty plates that had held their supper sat beside the lamp. Longarm was occupying the room's only chair, while Graciada sat on the cot. She was leaning back on her elbows, her long black hair cascading over her shoulders and framing her face.

"Yes, the cave is very quiet when the men are away delivering a shipment," she agreed. "But I have stayed behind before, when everyone else went to the border with the mule train."

"You don't ever go with El Gato when he takes the powder to deliver, then?"

Graciada shook her head. "I have no one outside to visit, my father and mother are both dead. Almost all the men who work with El Gato have wives or *novias* where they will be going. I have no place with them there."

"And you don't get lonesome when they're gone, all by yourself in this big place?"

"There is always something new to see." She gestured toward the lamp, saying, "I take one of the *bombes* and go deep into the cavern. There are wonderful places in it, Longarm."

"I saw a couple of real fancy places myself, moseying around while El Gato and his crew were working," Longarm replied.

"If you go deeper into the cavern you will find chambers so big that the light does not shine across them. I do not go in those, for unless the light reaches across such a big cavern and shows a wall, you can stay lost there forever. Two of the men who once worked here have vanished in the cave."

"And you couldn't find them?"

Graciada shook her head. "For days we searched and called, but they did not hear us or could not answer. At last we had to give up. But all of us have been more careful since then."

"It's a lot bigger'n I figured, then."

"It is not to be believed," she went on. "There are big rooms where shining spears hang from the ceiling and sparkle like great diamonds and pearls when the light touches them, and other chambers where huge glistening pillars rise from the floor, or where even the floor itself shines as if it had been spread with precious gems."

"I'll have to take another look around before I leave. I sure ain't ever seen anything like this cave before."

"When my foot has healed more, I will be glad to show you some of the places in it that I have discovered," Graciada offered. "We have nothing else to do while we wait for El Gato and the men to come back."

"El Gato said they'll be gone about a week."

"Or even a bit more," she said with a nod. "They will not reach the border for three days, then if all goes well they will rest a day before they start back."

Longarm was silent for a moment or two, then he remarked, "It ain't none of my business, but ever since I saw you I've been wondering about you, Graciada."

"Wondering what?"

"How you happened to get wound up in this powder-making thing with El Gato," Longarm replied. "You're a cut above most of the others that work down here."

"It is no secret," she said. "My father was the youngest son of my grandparents, who came here with the Emperor Maximiliano. After the emperor was executed by Diaz, Father joined Lerdo's forces and was killed by Diaz's troops at Tecoac."

"So your family sorta got busted up," Longarm commented when Graciada paused.

"De verdad," she agreed. "My mother had no money, then no place to go. She took me with her and joined the other refugees. El Gato was one of them; he had also been on Lerdo's side. He formed his band soon after my mother died, and I went with them."

"Well, now," Longarm told her, "I ain't much on knowing about all the generals and kings and presidents that've been in and out down here, that was on the top and got shot off of it. But I reckon I can figure out a lot you didn't tell me from what you said. So you're El Gato's woman."

"No!" Graciada protested. "I am my own woman! I do not belong to anyone, Longarm!"

"Maybe that's the best way to be," Longarm told her.

"I sorta like not being tied to apron strings myself."

"Then we are of a kind, you and me. And I have not yet thanked you enough for coming to help me when I was trapped outside the other day. There has never been time, we have been so busy."

"Why, you ain't got nothing to thank me for, Graciada," he protested. "It'd've been the same if there'd been somebody else but you cornered out there."

"Even so, it was me you came to help," she replied. "Take the light and put it out in the passage, Longarm. The thanks I would give you are better offered in the dark."

For a moment Longarm was tempted to refuse, but he had been on a rough and trying road for several weeks. Graciada was leaning forward now. Her full breasts were pressing against her dress, their tips thrusting against its thin fabric, the cleft between them a dark, inviting mystery. The flame of the lamp was reflected in her shining eyes, her lips full and glistening, inviting him.

Longarm did not protest further. He carried the lamp into the passageway and set it on the stone floor, then returned to the chamber. Graciada had undressed while he was gone and was lying on the narrow bed. Her upturned face was an oval broken only by the luminous shining pools of her eyes and the slash of her full lips. Longarm did not delay, but levered out of his boots and placed his gun belt on the floor beside the narrow cot. Then he wasted no time in shedding his shirt and trousers and balbriggans and stepping up to the bed.

Graciada lay looking up at him. She said, "You are much man, Longarm, and I have not been with a man for many weeks. Come and lie with me."

Longarm stretched out beside her on the bed. She

turned a bit to press herself against him and he pulled her to him, feeling the warmth of her body, soft and muscular at the same time. Then her hands were on him, muscular hands, rubbing and squeezing and demanding. Longarm half turned to get closer to her, and Graciada threw her leg across his hips and positioned him at once.

When Longarm moved and went into her she sought his lips with hers. Then he began thrusting slowly and regularly, and as he continued his shallow rhythmic thrusts he felt Graciada's body begin trembling gently. He did not speed his lunges, but moved with long-spaced deliberation to prolong the sensation for each of them. Their lips clung together and their tongues entwined as he kept up the gentle rhythm.

Time slipped away and neither Longarm nor Graciada noticed the minutes. At last she began trembling more violently. She pulled him closer to her, rotating her shoulders now and then to scrape the firmed tips of her breasts against his matted muscular chest.

Suddenly Longarm felt her quiver. He stopped his thrusting and held her quietly until the tremor faded and passed. When she lay motionless again he resumed his steady thrusts, but with more vigor now. Soon Graciada's hips began to roll in response to Longarm's strokes. She brought her legs up higher and her body grew taut. Longarm kept up his steady rhythm until Graciada started moaning deep in her throat, then he speeded up.

He plunged now, going into her deeply and quickening the tempo of his lunges. Soon Graciada was responding as vigorously as Longarm was stroking. She met his thrusts with quick twisting movements of her hips, raising them to meet him each time he buried himself with a full downward plunge. Her moans became a wordless throaty chant that echoed through the small darkened room.

Suddenly Graciada cried out sharply as her body jerked and quivered. Her chant became staccato ululations that filled the underground chamber with sounds that resonated and echoed off the stone walls. Longarm was also reaching the point of no return. He increased the pace of his thrusts until Graciada cried out in a final climactic scream, and after a final few desperate lunges he quivered and jetted. Then he dropped inert on Graciada's soft, pulsating body, and the only sound that filled the chamber was the rasping of their exhausted breathing. After a while they slept.

"This is a good day for me to show you some of the wonders I have found here in the cave," Graciada told Longarm.

During the days that had passed since their first experience at discovering each other, she and Longarm had settled into a smoothly happy relationship. As Graciada's foot healed, they spent much of their time going outside the cave for brief intervals, though they were careful never to go too far from the mouth, and kept a close watch on the surrounding countryside during their brief rambles.

Equally as much, they took pleasure in plunging from daylight to darkness, and in sharing the darkness in bed. Even now they were not sure whether it was day or night outside. All that mattered at the moment was that they had the huge cavern to themselves.

"Well, I ain't one to say no to anything a lady wants, so if you got a mind to wander in the dark, that's just what we'll do," Longarm agreed.

"We will need my string, and some candles," she said. "The lanterns are too big and heavy to carry with us."

"What about the string?" Longarm asked.

"We will need it when we go into places I have not yet been. I can find my way around in the passageways and chambers that I've already explored, but we must be sure we will be able to find our way out when we go into new ones that are strange."

Armed with string and rope, candles and matches, Longarm and Graciada began their exploration. Graciada led him first along a wide and lofty stone-floored corridor to what at first glance seemed a mere crack in the wall.

"We must squeeze through," she told him. "But once we are inside you will see something you have never seen before."

Longarm waited for Graciada to slip sideways through the high fissure, then followed her. It was a tight squeeze—his chest brushed one edge of the crack and his back was pressed tightly against the opposite edge—but he managed to slide through the opening. Then he blinked his eyes unbelievingly, for the countless thousands of brilliant needlepoints of light thrown back by the flame of Graciada's single candle stabbed at them with an intensity that was almost painful.

From the walls, floor, and high, domed ceiling where they originated, the narrow lines of brilliance lanced into Longarm's eyes. The light of the single candle that Graciada was holding high was multiplied and magnified an uncountable number of times, and each time Graciada's arm moved the lines moved with it. When Longarm's eyes had adjusted to the unexpected brightness, he tried to take in the full effect of the display, but its very magnitude made his effort useless.

"Them little crystals in the wall look like diamonds," he told her. "You reckon they could be?"

"Unfortunately, they are only mica or quartz or some soft stone," she said. "I had the same thought when I first saw them, but when I tried the little bright stones with the point of my knife they broke easily."

"Too bad. They'd sure make a man rich, if they were."

"I'm afraid the richness is only in their looks," she said. "But let's move on. There is another such chamber only a short distance from here."

There was no need for Longarm to squeeze into the next branch off the main passageway. Even before they reached it, the flickering candle brought bright darting shafts reflected from the uncountable thousands of slender spearheads that descended from the high arch of the new chamber's tall ceiling.

A few of the larger spearheads had reached the floor to form an hourglass shape between it and the lofty arch above. Even fewer had grown into columns thicker than a man's chest, and gave the illusion that they were furnishing the high dome's support. From them the candle's flicker also brought reflected rays of colored light, though the reflections were not as brilliant and varied as those in the room they'd just visited.

"I've seen a lot of things while I was knocking around the country in my job," Longarm remarked, shaking his head, "but I got to admit it, I've never seen anything that'll match this place."

"Nor have I," she agreed. "And there is still much more that I have not shown you, rooms and passageways that I have not wanted to risk entering alone. Now that you are with me, I will not have such fear."

"Well, lead on," Longarm told her. "We got nothing but time on our hands till El Gato and the others get back. As long as we get back to where we started in time for supper, we might as well look at everything that's down here."

"Always before when I have waited for El Gato and the men to return, I have been impatient to see them once more," Graciada told Longarm as they sat at supper. After the long day spent exploring the cave, they'd been contented to eat cold tortillas and cheese when they returned to the gunpowder-making area. "Now I find myself wanting for us to be here alone longer."

"I'd like that myself," Longarm told her. "But they're already a day late, the way you figure. You don't reckon something's happened to 'em, do you?"

"They are in danger during any trip they make into Mexico," she replied. "But until we have waited another day or two, I will not worry. All I think of now is that when they get back, you will leave."

"I still got my job to do," Longarm reminded her. "Don't forget, I was sent down here to find out about Geronimo and his Apaches. El Gato was going to bring me some leads on 'em if he could dig out any. If he does, I'm going to have to get busy and follow 'em up right away."

"If El Gato does as he planned, there will be another shipment of gunpowder for him to deliver soon. Less than a week will be needed for the men to fill the few bags that are now empty."

"You figure he'll want to make two trips so close together? My grandma back in West Virginia used to say something about the pitcher that went to the well too many times generally being the one that got busted first."

Graciada shook her head and said, "El Gato is too smart for the rurales. He does not follow the same path each trip. Sometimes he goes across the river north of El Paso, sometimes to the south. Sometimes he goes straight, sometimes in a circle."

"But the rurales know where the cave is now," Longarm reminded her.

"And they also know that it is not in Mexico, but in the United States," she pointed out. "They will not risk attacking us again."

"I wouldn't put it past—" Longarm broke off as a man's voice, unrecognizable in the echoes that reverberated with it, came from the cave's entrance. Springing to his feet, Longarm's hand dropped to the butt of his Colt as he said, "Now, that could be El Gato coming back even if it don't sound like him."

"It must be, though. We know he should be here by now."

"I grant you that, Graciada. But if it ain't, then it means we got strange company, and the way things sit right now, strange company generally means trouble. You wait here. I'll go take a look-see."

Graciada was already reaching for her rifle. "We will go together. If it is El Gato and the men, we have lost nothing. If it is the rurales returning, we will face them together."

Longarm held the bulbous, old-fashioned railroad lantern high in his left hand as he and Graciada walked side by side down the corridor and through the big, high-arched workroom. As they reached the wide passageway that led to the cave mouth, a babble of voices reached them from the outside.

Longarm stopped and placed the lantern on the stone floor. "We better go the rest of the way in the dark," he said. "If it ain't El Gato, we'd be sitting ducks carrying a light."

Moving more slowly now, he and Graciada continued their advance. They got into the night-dark entranceway just as two men came into it. They were black, unrecognizable silhouettes against the starshine of the night outside.

Longarm drew his Colt. Beside him, Graciada levered a shell into the magazine of her rifle. Then a man's voice broke the stillness.

"It's a hell of a lot bigger than I thought it'd be," he said. "And darker than the hinges of hell."

Longarm relaxed. As he holstered his Colt he said to Graciada, "It's El Gato, all right."

"But that was not his voice!" she protested.

"No. But it's a voice I'd know any place on earth. That's my boss, Billy Vail."

Chapter 10

Longarm had started taking long strides toward the cave's entrance the moment he recognized Billy Vail's voice. Now he called, "Billy! Billy Vail! What in the hell are you doing here?"

"For one thing, I'm looking for you," Vail replied. By now he and Longarm were close enough together for them to speak in normal tones.

"Well, I'd sure say you found me without too much trouble," Longarm observed. By this time he'd reached Vail's side and grabbed the hand the chief marshal was extending. The arms of the two men pumped vigorously for a moment, then Longarm went on, saying, "But how'd you get connected up with El Gato?"

"I might've been holding down a desk for a long time," Vail said blandly, "but I haven't forgotten all of the tricks I learned while I was working in the field. You know as well as I do that if you know anything about the man you're after, a few questions in the right places will turn him up for you fast."

Longarm nodded and agreed. "Yep. I been through

enough to've found out that. But what's brought you all the way down here, Billy? I hope it wasn't just to find me."

"Let's put off talking about that for a while," Vail said. "Just like I'm going to put off asking you any questions until later. But you'd better be thinking about how you'll answer me when I do start asking."

"Whatever you say, Billy," Longarm agreed. "But I guess you know I'm plumb glad to see you. You're looking good."

"You don't look like you've missed many meals yourself." Vail smiled, then his nose wrinkled and he asked, "What in the hell is it that I keep smelling?"

"Batshit, Billy. Seems like there's about a million of 'em that live in this cave. But don't worry, you'll get used to it, just like I did. After you've been here a while you'll forget that this place is likely the biggest stink-hole in the world."

"That's one thing you've said that I'll agree with, about it being a stinkhole. But right now, about all I want to do is find a place to spread out my bedroll and bunk. I haven't been away from my desk long enough to get used to forking a horse all night, especially over country as rough as this is."

"Well, you sure won't have trouble finding enough room to bunk down in," Longarm assured him. "This cave is so damned big you could put the whole Denver Federal Building in it and have room enough for the Brown Palace Hotel and most of the buildings on Colfax Avenue to boot."

"Show me where to put my bedroll, then," Vail said. "All I need is an hour or so. Then we can have a talk in private."

Dodging in and out between the men who were still

unloading supplies from the mule train, Longarm led Vail to the small cavern that El Gato used for his office and living quarters. As soon as the chief marshal had spread his bedroll and crawled into it, Longarm left Vail to sleep and sought El Gato. He found the ex-rurale supervising the men as they unloaded the mules.

"Chief Marshal Vail doesn't seem to've had any trouble running you to ground," he told El Gato. "But how in tunket did he talk you into bringing him here?"

"Your Chief is a very persuasive man, Longarm. And he also has ways of finding out things. He needed to use very few words to convince me that you would benefit from talking with him, and that you would bear me no ill will for bringing him here."

"I ain't a bit mad at you for doing it, Gato. If it was a case of push coming to shove, I'm sorta glad to see him. And you can bet a peso to a plugged nickel that if it hadn't been something real important, Billy wouldn't've come all this way looking for me."

"Then you are not angry?"

"Not one bit."

"If that is so, I am glad I did what he asked me to. If I had not agreed, we might have found our powder making finished."

"You mean Billy was ready to close you down if you didn't tell him where I was?"

"No. It was the Mexican government that made that threat, not him. But in return for bringing him here, he has told me something that could have meant a great deal of trouble later, if I had not known it."

"Now you got my curiosity all roused up again," Longarm said, frowning. "What was it he told you?"

"You will hear it from Marshal Vail soon enough, so I may as well tell you now. Diaz has complained to your government that we are using United States territory to make powder to fight against the Mexican government. He has even threatened to begin a new war against your country if we do not stop making gunpowder in the cavern."

"You mean you're getting put outa business? But if you quit making powder, what's going to become of your friends who're fighting Diaz? How will they get the powder they need?"

"Bat guano is the main ingredient on which our powder making depends, Longarm," El Gato said. "There was nothing said that will keep us from hauling the guano across the border. And on the Mexican side of the Rio Grande it will be much easier to deliver the powder to our friends who need it, our *insurgentes*."

"That's what you aim to do, then?"

"Of course. We have a small stock of powder that we did not have enough mules to haul on the trip we just made. We will work here a few more days, until we have another full load, then we will take the powder and our bits and pieces of equipment into the Sierra Oriental. In the mountains there we will be making powder once again within two or three weeks."

"You don't think the rurales will stop you?"

"Oh, they will try, of course. But that will be nothing new. We have fought them before and won."

"You know, Gato, if I didn't have another kettle of fish to fry, I'd sure be tempted to go along and help you. But Billy Vail's come all this way to tell me something new about the job I set out to do, and I got to tend to that."

"Well, Billy, now that you've caught up with your sleep, I guess it's time for us to talk," Longarm said.

He and Billy Vail were sitting alone in the cavern used by El Gato as his bedroom. Though still a bit red-eyed from his recent sleepless nights, Vail seemed to be himself again.

"It's way past time," he told Longarm. "Dammit, Long, once you get out of sight, you're a hell of a hard man to catch up with."

"How'd you catch up to me, anyhow?"

"You keep forgetting that I didn't put in all my time as a marshal sitting at a desk shuffling papers"—Vail smiled—"and I made a few friends in the Indian Bureau while I was working in the field. Of course, it'd've been easier for me to find you if you'd filed all the reports you're supposed to."

"Now, Billy, I've just been trying to do my job. You can't blame me if it's kept me hopping around so much I ain't had time to do a lot of scribbling," Longarm protested.

"Seems to me I've heard that before," Vail said. "But once I got enough meat out of your reports I could figure that you'd have to stop in at Fort Bliss. It wasn't a big job to track you when you started out from Bliss and headed this way."

"It made sense to me, even if it don't to you. And the way things are turning out, I'd say I done the right thing."

"From what I've heard about the way you've been acting down here, you've stirred things up pretty good," Vail said. "In case it's slipped your mind, you're on detached service with the Indian Bureau, Long. How in hell did you come to get mixed up with El Gato and the rurales?"

"Why, I found out that El Gato was selling a little bit of gunpowder to Geronimo's outfit now and again,"

Longarm said. "I figured I might get a lead that I could follow from here. That's why I wound up being at this big stinkhole."

"You haven't reported any of this to the Indian Bureau yet," Vail snapped, "unless you've sent a report back east within the last few days. I sure hadn't heard about them getting anything from you before I left Denver."

"There just ain't been time for me to report in, Billy. It seems like every time I try to leave to find a telegraph office, something stops me. Like the other day, when the rurales jumped the border and came up here and tried to wipe El Gato's folks out. And I ain't heard enough about Geronimo to stuff in a doughnut hole."

"Well, I can give you a little bit of help there. You can forget about Geronimo, Long," Vail said. "He's already surrendered to General Crook."

Longarm's jaw dropped in surprise. "You mean he's quitting, plumb giving up?"

"That's what I picked up off the army's telegraph wire when I stopped at Fort Bliss on my way here," Vail explained. "The army's holding Geronimo and his whole bunch of Apache renegades at one of the little forts over in Arizona Territory. They're going to keep them there for a while, but nobody seems to know how long."

"If the army keeps fooling around with them Apaches, they're going to wind up with what the little boy shot at. From what I've seen of the army and what I've heard about Geronimo, the Apaches will stay put just about as long as it suits 'em to. Then they'll just sorta fade away and leave the army wondering what happened to 'em."

"They're not going to be held very long in Arizona

Territory from what I gathered," Vail said. "Just long enough for the army to fix up a place for them in Florida."

"Florida!" Longarm exclaimed.

"That's right. They're going to keep the Apaches in Florida, in one of the old forts left from the Seminole wars. They'll ship them east in a special train with army guards."

"Well, I wish 'em luck, Billy. Just the same, I don't figure to leave these parts till I see the soldiers herd them Apaches on the train that's taking 'em east. That breed of redskins is tricky as all hell, and I aim to be sure the army don't make no fool mistakes."

"What kind of mistakes could they make?"

"Now, Billy, you know what the army's like these days. A bunch of boys that's still wet behind the ears."

"I'll have to agree with you about that," Vail admitted. "They sure aren't like the men that served with Grant and Sherman or Lee and Stonewall Jackson."

"Most of 'em is right off a farm back east," Longarm went on, "where there ain't been no real wild Indians since before they were born. So that's why I aim to stick around here a little while longer."

"Doing what? Dammit, Long, you're supposed to be on that job for the Indian Bureau!"

"And that's what I'll be doing, Billy."

"Doing what?" Vail repeated. "Getting in the army's way? Maybe you'd better get down to cases."

"Why, I don't aim to do much except keep an eye on El Gato's outfit."

"I don't guess I follow you," Vail said, frowning.

"Why, I'd think you could see that right off, Billy. If Geronimo decides not to go to Florida, he'll make a break to get free from Crook's men. You know Apaches as well as I do. They got a way of just all of a sudden showing up where they ain't supposed to be, or maybe not being where everybody else figures they are. From what I've heard about Geronimo's bunch, they're about the trickiest of all of 'em."

"I see what you're getting at," Vail said. "If Geronimo changes his mind and manages to get his men away from the army, the first thing he'll need is gunpowder, so he'll come to El Gato to buy it."

"That's about the way I look at it," Longarm agreed. "It ain't that I'm hankering to tie into a passel of wild Apaches, Billy. I just hope we don't have to turn to and help the army round 'em up again."

"Even if Crook keeps the Apaches corralled, that doesn't finish your job with the Indian Bureau," Vail went on. "At least not the way I understand it. Wasn't there something in it about you taking a look at the Navahos after you'd finished down here?"

"Sure." Longarm nodded. "Soon as I finish this job here, I'm supposed to go up to Fort Sumner and get my new papers. Mr. Harrington's sending his orders through the army instead of the Indian Bureau. He said he didn't want them people that works for him to know why I'm snooping around."

"You're not going to have a lot to do while you're waiting," Vail said thoughtfully.

"Not a lot," Longarm agreed. "Except I figure to help El Gato move over to Mexico. That's one way I'll be sure of knowing where I can find him."

"I don't suppose you'd object to having some company?"

Longarm stared at Vail for a moment, then asked, "I guess you mean yourself, Billy?"

"You don't see anybody else around, do you?"

"What about the office?"

"It'll get along without me for a while. I put in for all the leave I've been piling up for the last two years. I guess you know that's how long I've been sitting behind that desk without any kind of relief."

"I knew it'd been a while, but I didn't know it'd been all that much time."

"Dammit, I've been doing nothing but shuffling papers for so long that I'm getting rusty!" Vail exclaimed. "For the last few months I've had a real hankering to get out of that office chair and on a horse again!"

"Well, I always say a man oughta do what he feels like doing," Longarm said. "But it ain't going to be much of a cakewalk, going with El Gato."

"I'm not asking for a turn around a honky-tonk's dance floor, dammit!" Vail shot back. "Give me credit for knowing what I might be getting into."

"Oh, I'm not saying a word against you doing what you feel like you want to," Longarm said quickly. "I figure if a man's got a hankering to do something, the best thing for him to do is go ahead and get it over with."

Vail nodded. "I'm glad we agree on that, Long."

"There's still one thing we might not agree on, though," Longarm went on. "I've heard you say lawmen ought not to fight each other, and there's more'n a half chance we might have to swap shots with Diaz's rurales. Over on the other side of the border, they're lawmen, and if—"

"Stop right there!" Vail broke in. "The rurales used to be lawmen, and damned good ones. But Diaz has changed all that. They're his own private army now,

Long, not any better than plain everyday bandits or hired guns."

"Well, it makes me feel better to hear you say that, Billy. I don't guess you've had a chance to talk to El Gato about this scheme, have you?"

"Not yet. I wanted to talk to you first."

"Why, I feel downright good about it, Billy. Come on. Let's go find El Gato and see what he's got to say."

After El Gato had heard Longarm and Vail explain their proposal, his usually saturnine face broke into a broad grin.

"You have talked between yourselves, I am sure," he told them. "The men I have are skilled in making powder, but few of them at fighting. You know I will welcome you to go with us when we move."

"We ain't just going along for the trip," Longarm said. "I guess you can figure out why we figure it'd be a good thing for us to travel with you for a spell."

"I have no new teeth to cut," El Gato said. "You know that if Geronimo should change his mind and return to Mexico, he will come to me for powder. After he pays for the powder, I do not care what might happen to him."

"We understand each other, then," Vail said. "We'll pull our weight along the way, don't worry about that."

"I would not look for anything else, Marshal Vail." El Gato nodded.

"All right, Gato," Longarm put in. "We got a deal, then. You tell us what to do, and we'll do it."

"My men can handle the burros," El Gato replied. "But few are skilled with weapons, though they are learning fast. And Graciada will go with us, of course. She will see to the food and such matters. But with the wonderful new gun you have, Longarm, I do not think we need to worry too greatly that we will not reach our destination. Our packing is almost finished."

"When do you plan to start, then?" Vail asked.

"Since we have no sad farewells to make, I see no reason to delay. If you and Longarm are ready, we will leave tomorrow."

Chapter 11

"How much farther you figure we'll have to go before we get to the border?" Longarm asked El Gato.

"Another half day after we halt tonight. If we get an early start tomorrow, we can cross the border into Mexico by noon."

"I reckon you figure to go right on without nooning anyplace tomorrow, then?"

"It will be better if we do," El Gato said, nodding. "There is always danger in a border-crossing into Mexico, amigo."

"Rurale patrols?"

El Gato nodded. "They patrol regularly, but usually in the very early morning or late in the day, near sunset. I do not want to have another fight with them, amigo."

"So we'll hit it in the middle of the day," Longarm agreed.

"It has always been the safest time in the past," El Gato said. "Where the land is barren for many miles on both sides, there are no trails nearby, and the place I have chosen is in my mind, it does not show as a trail on any map."

Longarm and El Gato were riding in advance of the little procession of two-wheeled burro-drawn wagons that was making its way slowly across some of the most desolate country Longarm could remember having seen. Almost a full week had gone by since they'd left what Longarm referred to—without any affection in his voice—as the big stinkhole, and headed west.

Two days of steady, slow, uneventful traveling had taken them to the Rio Grande, and three more days had passed since they'd crossed the border between New Mexico and Arizona Territory. They'd swung north of El Paso to avoid the settlement and Fort Bliss, which lay within a stone's throw of the growing little town.

After fording the Rio Grande above El Paso they'd advanced steadily westward. Only after passing within close sight of the forbidding black lava beds that made a huge black blot on the sunbaked ocher earth did El Gato order the *carretas* to turn to the south.

Now, great expanses of sunbaked yellowish soil stretched away from them in all directions. There was no road ahead, only the baked, barren, unmarked earth. Behind them stretched the twin churned and broken parallel ruts made by the wheels of the deep-bodied, burro-drawn *carretas*. One of the stubby, primitive, two-wheeled wagons contained the party's personal belongings, the other two piled high with the few pieces of equipment that was necessary to start powder making. The workbenches and mixing buckets and other gear had been lashed on top of a supply of bat guano, which El Gato had assured them would be enough to last at least a month.

Graciada sat on the bits of bedding and bags of personal belongings, chiefly clothing, which were piled atop the load of the lead *carreta*. She and Longarm had managed only occasional moments together during the trip, for El Gato had proved to be an efficient and firm leader. The wagons rolled from daybreak until the after-sunset darkness made travel impossible, and after such long days of travel under the pitiless sun there was neither time nor energy for anything but a short night's sleep.

Longarm, turning to glance back along the little procession after his brief talk with El Gato, caught Graciada's eyes on him and wheeled his horse up to the *carreta*.

"It's a hot rough trip, but El Gato just told me we oughta get to wherever it is we're heading by noon tomorrow," he told her. "Maybe then we can find a little bit of time to ourselves."

"More than likely we'll be too busy getting everything ready to start making powder again," she replied.

"Oh, I reckon he won't waste much time getting started. But I found out back there in the cave that you can't make powder without water. From what I've seen in this desert country around here, wherever there's water there's trees or at least bushes we can duck into."

"Just not having to ride on this *carreta* in the burning sunshine anymore will make me happy," she said. "But I do miss being with you."

"Likewise," he said. "We'll talk some more this evening when we stop, Graciada. Right now, I got to ride back and see how my friend's holding up."

Billy Vail was holding up much better than Longarm had expected for a man who'd been desk-bound such a long time. His face had turned red soon after the beginning of the trip and had glowed for several days, but now the red had changed tone and had become a healthy tan. He greeted Longarm with a wave and a cheerful smile.

"This is the medicine I've been needing," he said as Longarm reached him and wheeled his horse around to ride beside him. "Why, I've been so busy cussing this damned hot sun and the heat and all that I haven't even had time to miss my desk and swivel chair back in Denver."

"You figure you got enough leave time left to stick around a little bit longer, then?" Longarm asked.

"Plenty. From what El Gato said this morning, we'll be wherever it is we're headed sometime tomorrow. I imagine you'll want to do a little scouting around and learn the lay of the land and all that, so I planned on riding with you."

"Why, I'll be glad for company, Billy. But El Gato says he knows that part of Mexico pretty well," Longarm replied. "If there's some kind a hidey-hole where a bunch of rurales might be holed up, he'll either go along while we give it a look or he'll tell us where to head."

"Either way," Vail said, "count on me for company."

"Sure, Billy," Longarm said, nodding. "It's been a while since me and you was out working a case together. I reckon it'll do us both good."

Noon had passed by an hour or more the following day and the constant hot wind that had rippled across the baked yellow sandy soil was dying away when El Gato waved for the leading *carreta* to rein in at the crest of a long tiring rise. He studied the ground behind them for a moment, then turned his attention to the long downslope that stretched ahead. After that he looked for a moment and motioned for the others to halt.

122

Longarm had been riding a bit ahead of the three wagons. He'd already started down the slope when the creaking and squeaking of the *carretas* died away. He turned in the saddle to look back and saw that the little procession had stopped, and saw also that El Gato was sitting his horse beside the lead wagon, waving. Reining around, he went back to join the group. By the time Longarm reached El Gato's wagon, Billy Vail had come up from the rear of the little procession to join them.

"Something wrong?" Longarm asked El Gato.

El Gato shook his head and said, "Nothing yet. But our talk yesterday set me to thinking. We have been traveling for several days, always at the same slow speed. If I can predict when we will cross the border, others can, too."

"You mean the rurales," Longarm suggested.

"Of course. You have learned their ways a bit, and I have learned them very well indeed, or I would not still be alive."

"I'd say you've got something in mind," Vail told him.

"Of course," El Gato said. "All of us know the rurales are not the strutting fools some people take them for. On a long trip such as we have made, they have had too many chances to watch us without being seen."

"There's something besides that," Vail put in. "They'd be less likely to've jumped us on the American side of the border than they will be from now on."

"True," El Gato agreed, then said, "Longarm, I would like for you and Billy to ride with me while we do a small bit of scouting."

"You don't reckon it's too risky, leaving the wagons?"

"Graciada can manage them. It is only a short way to

123

the place where we will stop, and she knows the country as well as I do," El Gato said. "She has her rifle, and is very good at using it. Two of the *jovenes* also have good guns, but I do not know how skilled they are with them."

"When I was a just a kid back in West Virginia, I heard my grandpa say something that's always stuck in my mind," Longarm remarked. "He said a younker learning how to shoot don't really learn to aim quick and true until he's shooting back at somebody that's aiming to kill him. I don't reckon you need to fret much about your young fellows, Gato. Chances are they'll do whatever it is they got to."

"It is a risk worth taking," El Gato said decisively. "We will move the wagons down to that break"—he pointed to a little ravine a few hundred yards ahead— "and then the three of us will fan out and ride a large circle around the trail."

"What trail?" Vail asked.

He waved a hand at the vast expanse of yellow sandy soil that surrounded them. Its surface was broken only by a few rippled areas created by the wind and by an occasional clump of thick-stalked *saguaro* mixed with more extensive stands of sparse-branched and equally spiny cholla. Nowhere on the floor of the desert did the baked sand crust show any signs of hoofprints or wagon ruts.

"There is a trail of sorts," El Gato replied. "But you must have desert-trained eyes to see it, Billy. Look behind you and see if you can make out our trail, amigo."

Vail stood up in his stirrups and looked behind him. The path taken by the wagons was clearly marked for a distance of perhaps a half or three quarters of a mile. Beyond that, the hot and gentle but persistent desert breeze had already rearranged the crust broken by the wagon wheels into the universal pattern of ripples that characterized the entire terrain.

"I've been doing all my riding in a desk chair too long," Vail said as he settled back into his saddle. "I never did spend a lot of time in desert country, anyhow. I'd forgotten about this wind, and how it hides tracks."

"There are a few rurales who are very skillful trackers," El Gato said as he led Longarm and Vail away from the *carretas*. "And even a good tracker will need a great deal of time to follow us, but that does not mean we have time to waste."

"How much farther do we have to go?" Longarm asked.

"Beyond the next ridge we reach a valley where there are two lakes," El Gato answered. "Laguna de Guzman and Laguna Santa Maria. They were once one, but that was long ago, before the memory of man. Between them runs a deep valley. It has a spring in it with sweet water for drinking, and the spring is very close to Laguna Santa Maria. We will carry water from it to use in making our powder."

"All we got to do is get there, then," Longarm said.

"Without the rurales stopping us," El Gato added. As he swept the horizon with a gesture he said, "Marshal Vail, if you will ride to the west, and you, Longarm, to the east, I will go straight over the ridge ahead, and between us we should be able to see if there is any danger near."

"How far you figure we oughta scout?" Longarm asked.

"No more than three or four miles. I will stop where we will make our workplace. The wagons will leave a good trail for you to follow there."

"We'll be settling in for a while, then?" Vail asked.

"Unless the rurales find us again and force us to move to a more hidden place," El Gato replied. "I'm sure they will be on our trail sooner or later, and they know this country almost as well as I do."

Separating, the three rode off. Longarm kept well below the crest of the ridge he was following, riding up cautiously to the crest only now and then to scan the terrain beyond. He'd covered half the distance mentioned by El Gato when he heard the distant nickering of a horse. Reining in, he sat quietly until the snorting nicker was repeated. Then he could hear the scraping of shod hooves beyond the gentle curve of a deep arroyo that cut between the ridges.

Jerking the reins, Longarm turned his horse downslope, rode a short distance, and dismounted. He slid his Winchester from its saddle scabbard and started back up the slope on foot. Before his head cut above the crest, he bent forward and dropped into a crouch to cover the short distance remaining. A yard or two from the top of the ridge he dropped to his knees and crawled the rest of the way on all fours. Near the rim, he flattened himself to the baked soil and wriggled forward on his belly until he could peer over the crest.

When Longarm looked down, he found that he was peering into the stone-strewn bed of what had once been a big creek or a small river. The long-dry streambed stretched along the floor of a shallow valley in a gentle curve, and the noises came from some point that was not yet visible beyond the sweep of the banks in which water had run long ago. Patiently, Longarm waited.

His patience was soon rewarded. The noises of the scraping hooves came steadily closer from beyond the old streambed's curve and then a horseman appeared.

The rider wore the style of sombrero favored by the rurales. It was midnight-black and had an over-wide brim with ornamentation stitched in gold. The crown also glinted with gold thread, and the charro jacket worn by the man was lavishly embroidered in elaborately swirling patterns formed by threads of mixed gold and silver.

"Looks like you got the answer El Gato was looking for, old son," Longarm muttered under his breath. "But the question is, has that fellow come all by himself, or has he got somebody else along?"

Patiently but tensely, Longarm waited while the rurale's horse carried the man closer to the bank from which Longarm was watching. The rider was scanning the surface of the sandy rock-studded bottom of the arroyo as he rode. It was obvious at once to Longarm that the rurale was looking for hoofprints, for he paid no attention to the canyon's sloping walls. Moving slowly and carefully, Longarm began inching the barrel of his rifle forward along his side, to have it ready if the rurale should glance up.

Totally unaware of Longarm's watching eyes, the rurale advanced. He was only twenty or thirty feet distant now, and Longarm began measuring with his eyes the distance the man still had to travel before the danger of being discovered would be past. Suddenly, from the narrow lip of a rock outcrop almost directly beneath his chin, a desert jay swooped out, its raucous chattering squawk breaking the silence.

Longarm and the rurale looked at the jay at almost the same instant. As the rurale raised his eyes and Longarm lowered his in automatic response to study the man's face, their eyes met for a fleeting instant. Then the rurale dropped the reins of his horse and his hand darted for his gun as Longarm started to level his rifle.

Swift as the reflexes of both men were, the jay was faster than either of them. It swooped down on the rurale, fluttering around his face and forcing him to raise both hands to protect his eyes from its long, needle-pointed stabbing beak. Longarm held his fire for a split second, debating whether to call on the rurale to surrender or to shoot.

His mental debate lasted only a few seconds. It ended when the rurale's hand reached the butt of his revolver and he started to draw. Before he could complete his move, Longarm triggered his rifle. The slug knocked the man out of his saddle. As he fell, his foot twisted in the stirrup and lodged there. His horse spurted forward, dragging its master's corpse. The desert jay had taken wing with a series of raucous squawks when the gunshots echoed along the canyon.

Longarm watched the horse as it disappeared around the curve in the canyon's walls. The rurale's foot was still caught firmly in the stirrup, his body bouncing along the hard-packed earth of the canyon as the animal galloped wildly ahead.

For a moment Longarm held his position, his rifle ready in the event the rurale had been only one member of a group sent to explore the area. When enough time had passed for him to be sure that the man had been alone, he remounted and rode as close as possible to the canyon wall, his eyes searching for the horse and the grisly burden it had been dragging. He covered more than a mile before he saw the animal. The rurale's body was stretched out beside its feet, the dead man's booted foot twisted firmly into the stirrup that had been his undoing.

Old son, Longarm told himself silently as he reined

in, *this ain't going to be a nice job, but it's one you got to do.*

He toed his horse ahead, looking for a place where the walls of the canyon sloped gently enough to allow him to ride down into the deep gulch. Almost a mile from the spot where the rurale's horse had stopped he found the place he'd been seeking. He slid his mount down the slope and rode back along the bed of the long-dry stream until he reached the horse and the battered body of its rider. The hard-baked soil of the canyon and the rocks embedded in it had done their work; the rurale's face was not something pleasant to look on.

Setting his jaw, Longarm searched the dead rurale's pockets, but found nothing except a few silver pesos and some smaller coins, a sack of tobacco and some cornhusks trimmed for rolling into cigarettes. The saddlebags on the horse were more rewarding. There was a thick sheaf of papers with handwritten Spanish, and a sizable leather sack heavy with gold and silver coins.

Longarm restored what he'd found to the saddlebags before hoisting the unwieldy body of the rurale across his horse. Then, with the dead man's lariat as a lead rope, he mounted his own horse. Leading the rurale's horse, he started back to join his companions.

Chapter 12

Dusk was beginning to settle in by the time Longarm reached the place where he and Vail and El Gato had separated and ridden away from the wagons. There was enough light left in the steadily deepening blue of the cloudless sky for him to see the fresh ruts left by the *carretas,* however. He nudged his mount ahead, and with his burden still in tow set out to follow the wagon ruts over the arid rolling country that stretched in front of him.

He'd ridden only a mile or so when he saw Billy Vail angling cross-country toward the road. Vail saw Longarm at about the same time, and waved. Longarm reined in and lighted one of his long slim cigars. He puffed it while he sat in the saddle and waited for Vail to join him.

"Looks like you picked up a load somewhere," Vail said as he got within easy speaking distance. Then as he pulled up beside Longarm, he was silent for a moment while his eyes flicked over the horse and its motionless rider. Then he said, "And by what's left of the outfit that dead man's got on, I'd say he was a rurale."

"He sure was. We butted heads together in a draw a ways back," Longarm answered.

"You didn't see any more of 'em?"

Longarm shook his head. "Just him. Close as I could make out, he was trying to track down our wagons."

"And getting pretty close, I'd say."

"Too close for comfort," Longarm agreed. "I didn't set out to kill him, but he spotted me, and knowing what the rurales act like, I figured I didn't have much choice but to shoot first. So that's what I did."

"Looks like you used that quick-firing gun, too, the way he's all torn up," Vail commented.

"Don't go blaming me for how he looks, Billy. I put a rifle bullet in him, all right, but I didn't have nothing to do with what happened after that. Fact of the matter is, he got scuffed up that way when he fell off his horse and got his foot caught in his stirrup. Then the horse drug him a ways before I could catch up to him."

"It's not often that you'll see a rurale alone," Vail said, frowning.

"No, but I figured like you, Billy. My guess is that him being out scouting around likely means there's more of 'em someplace close by."

"Sure"—Vail nodded—"from what I've seen of the rurales, they run in packs, like coyotes."

"And smell about as bad," Longarm commented. "But I didn't bring him back with me just so's we could bury him, Billy. His saddlebags have got a lot of papers in 'em that you and me and El Gato might find right interesting."

"I'd say El Gato'd be more interested than we are, Long. Whatever kind of revolution or trouble he's mixed up in is way outside U.S. territory."

"Sure. Except that right now we happen to be in

Mexican territory, and we better be interested in keeping out of the way of them rurales."

"I suppose," Vail admitted. "But it's a little bit hard for me to get used to the idea that I've got to stay out of the way of a lawman, crooked or not. And I still don't see how you got mixed up with El Gato again. You're on the Indian Bureau payroll right now, and I don't know of any Indians down here on the Mexican side of the border that they're interested in."

"You don't need to push that out in front of me, Billy. I've already told you what I'm doing down here."

Vail was silent for a moment, then he said, "I guess I was out of line a minute ago, Long. It sort of slipped my mind that you're not working out of my office in Denver right now. Let's both forget about it and head for wherever it is we're supposed to meet El Gato."

"Whatever you say, Billy. But if I recall right, El Gato went on the same way the wagons were heading. I figure all we got to do is follow the wheel tracks. If we do that, we'll likely catch up with him sooner or later."

"Better sooner than later," Vail said. "You know, Long, I've got a hunch your guess is right. I don't think this rurale you tangled with was the only one around here. Knowing how they work, it wouldn't surprise me a bit to find some of that fellow's friends prowling around here, looking for us."

"I wouldn't mind finding them," Longarm said. "As long as they don't see us first, which is what's likely to happen if we don't move along. Come on, Billy, let's ride."

In spite of the recurring skittishness of the horse carrying the dead rurale's body, Longarm and Vail made good time as they followed the ruts of the *carretas*. The road, more trail than road, ran reasonably straight until they

133

reached the lake El Gato had mentioned. Then it paralleled the shoreline, taking them east rather than south, until it suddenly vanished in a broad, gravel-filled wash, the course of some long-dry creek or small river.

"Well, there's just one thing that could've happened, Billy," Longarm told Vail as they reined in after having searched the dead streambed for a half mile in each direction.

"What's that?"

"El Gato knows this country pretty good, and he's about as cagey as they come. I got a hunch he just had them fellows in the wagons drive right down this old riverbed to the lake."

"I rode down by it almost to the lake," Vail objected. "And I didn't see hide nor hair of them."

"Neither did I in the other direction," Longarm replied. "But they damn sure didn't just sprout wings and fly off. Let's ride a ways farther toward the lake, on past where you stopped, and take another look-see."

Gravel grating under the hooves of their horses, they rode down the dry streambed. They passed the point where Vail had turned back, the lake still almost a mile away, and still had found no sign of the *carretas* when El Gato appeared in front of them in the riverbed, waving for them to pull up.

"Where the devil did you come from, Gato?" Longarm asked as he and Vail reached his side and reined up their mounts. "You got a rabbit hole someplace around here that you just dive in and out of?"

"Not a rabbit hole"—El Gato grinned—"but a place almost as good." He looked at the third horse with its burden and said, "Did this one jump you while you were looking for the place where the *carretas* were?"

"He sorta tried to," Longarm replied. "But he was just a mite slow when he went to draw."

"Why did you bring him here?" El Gato asked.

"Well, now," Longarm answered, "Billy and me didn't feel like waiting around till his friends came looking for him, and we didn't have time to dig him a grave. Besides, we sorta figured you might like to have a look at the papers that I found in his saddlebags."

"What kind of papers?" El Gato frowned.

"Letters of some sort," Vail said. "All in Spanish, of course, so we couldn't read them. I looked at one or two; they seemed to be orders from Mexico City. I didn't take time to try to go through everything, of course."

"There's a bag of money in there that you might find useful, too," Longarm put in. "I guess by right it belongs to the rurales, but knowing what I do about 'em, I'd bet they stole it from somebody."

"Money is always useful, amigo," El Gato said. "No matter where it comes from. And I like best the money that comes from our enemies." He went to the rurale's horse and took hold of its headstall, then said, "I will lead you to the new place where we will be working. It is not far from here."

Less than fifty yards from where they started, El Gato led Longarm and Vail into a branch of the dry streambed. The channel was neither as wide nor as deep as the one they'd just left, but like it, stretches of gravel lined its bottom. They walked for perhaps two hundred yards before entering an area where there were skeletons of trees. Their leafless branches spread over neatly spaced rows formed by the crisscrossing of ditches that formed a checkerboard pattern that covered several acres. The streambed they'd been following slanted upward here, its banks level with the horses' bellies.

"This is somebody's old orchard," Vail observed, looking at the rows of uniformly spaced trees. "I guess whoever put it in just pulled up stakes and moved away when the river dried up."

"Your guess is right, amigo," El Gato said. "There are many such places in this part of Mexico. My family had such an orchard as this when my father was a boy. He used to speak of it and how the little stream they depended on for water stopped flowing and forced them to move."

"And they just up and left?" Longarm asked.

El Gato shrugged. "What else could they do? Like the family this one belonged to, they took only their possessions. So, we will use for our powder making what remains of the house that the people who once lived here deserted."

Through the tree skeletons Longarm and Vail could now see the crumbling adobe walls of what had once been an expansive house. Moving around inside, the youths who'd come from the cavern were busy preparing the place for work. Longarm got only a fleeting glimpse of Graciada, who was bustling around gesturing at the young men who were doing the work inside the ruined dwelling.

"We will go inside without waiting to look around," El Gato said. "I am impatient to see what there is in the letters you mentioned." He was taking the saddlebags off the rurale's horse as he spoke. "I will have my people bury the rurale later, when they have finished the work they are now doing. There are already two graves on the other side of the house, so a third will draw little notice. Come, amigos, let us go and look into these saddlebags."

At first, Longarm had a feeling that walking through the deserted roofless house with its crumbling adobe walls was a bit like entering a dwelling that had been shaken to pieces by an earthquake, but the sensation soon vanished. He and Vail followed El Gato to what had once been a large living room. An adobe fireplace occupied one corner, the hearth half full of cracked and broken bricks. Through the glassless windows another dead orchard plot was visible, and beyond it the heat haze shimmered over ragged, featureless sandy soil, hiding the details of the terrain from them.

El Gato motioned to the floor and said, "Make yourselves as comfortable as possible. If we stay here, someday we may have chairs and tables to replace those we could not bring from the big cave."

"Well, at least you got a place that ain't a stinkhole," Longarm told him. "This ain't the first time I've sat on the floor, and I don't reckon it'll be the last."

El Gato had already opened one of the saddlebags and had taken out the bag of money. He set it aside and dumped the remaining contents on the floor. There seemed to be little except sheafs of folded papers, and he began to unfold each one in turn and scan it quickly. Sometimes he made a brief comment to give Longarm and Vail a hint of what the documents contained.

"A roster of the dead man's rurale company . . . a note from a girl in Ciudad Chihuahua . . . a notice of a reward for a murderer named Mateo Lantasan . . . a—" He stopped and began rereading the sheets of paper he'd just unfolded, then turned to Longarm and Vail.

"This is most interesting," he said, frowning. "It has to do with your country. It is an urgent notice from the headquarters of the rurales, and was sent out only four days ago. I will translate it for you. Listen, amigos."

Reading slowly, El Gato translated:

Our agents—this means spies working for your country, of course—report that the Apache Indian chief Geronimo has escaped with a number of his warriors, perhaps as many as twenty, from the custody of United States General Crook at Fort Huachuca. It is of a certainty that Geronimo has come into Mexico and he is now on our nation's soil south of the United States province of Arizona.

Because of the unfortunate attitude shown by the United States toward our country, President Diaz has agreed with out commandant's suggestion to refuse permission for forces of the United States military to cross the border if they should make such an effort as they pursue Geronimo. Should the men under your command encounter Geronimo and his Indians, you will provide them with rations and ammunition at their request.

If your unit should meet with any detachments of the United States military that have invaded Mexican soil to pursue these Apaches, you will order them to return to their own country and will escort them to the border to make sure that your command is obeyed. You must also make an immediate report to this office if such an incident should take place.

El Gato looked up from the report and raised his eyebrows at Longarm and Vail. He said, "I do not wish to offend you, my friends, but it seems that something has gone very badly amiss with your army."

"You ain't hurting my feelings none," Longarm replied instantly. "I ain't ever met up with this General Crook, but I've seen a lot of the damn army. It sure ain't what it used to be when General Grant was running things."

"Crook's just let himself be outsmarted," Vail said slowly. "It happens now and again. But from what I know about the way the army handles things, Crook's already been relieved and somebody else, some other general that gets things done, is out after Geronimo right now."

"Geronimo would not stay in your country, Billy," El Gato said. "He is more than likely in Mexico by now."

"Likely," Vail agreed. "And from that order you just read, your rurales aim to see that he don't get caught again."

"If the rurales do as they have been ordered, there is not much chance that he will," El Gato agreed.

"Well, it ain't no business of ours," Longarm said. "What we better do—"

"Hold on, Long!" Vail broke in. "Anything Geronimo does is the business of the Indian Bureau. And just in case it's slipped your mind, you're on their pay roster now."

"Danged if that occurred to me, Billy!" Longarm exclaimed. "I guess I just ain't in the habit yet of taking orders from anybody but you."

"I can't give you any orders," Vail said. "And don't intend to. I'm on leave, anyhow."

"No, but you got something working in your mind," Longarm told him. "I been around you long enough to know that."

"Call it habit," Vail said, shrugging.

"Trot it out and lay it on the table, Billy," Longarm said. "There won't either one of us feel right if you got something sticking in your craw."

"Well, you don't like the rurales any better than I do," Vail said.

"And I like them less than you or Longarm, Billy," El Gato broke in. "When I was a rurale, the force was

139

different. It was a body of volunteers, not the private army of our president and a few of his *rico* friends who think only of growing fatter by riding on the backs of the campesinos."

"Now, hold on," Longarm broke in. "I know what's been sticking in Billy's craw, and yours, too, Gato. And I guess I have to admit it, I've been thinking the same thing myself."

"Like I reminded you a minute ago, Long, you're drawing your pay from the Indian Bureau," Vail said.

"I ain't forgot, not since we got started on this string of palaver. Where the hell is this fort hoochy-koochy that was in them orders Gato read to us, Billy?"

Before Vail could answer, El Gato broke in, "Huachuca. It is to the west, in the corner of your Arizona Territory."

"Pretty close to Tombstone, then. Maybe a two-day ride if you're in a hurry." Longarm frowned. "Dry country, and rough as a cob, like all of it is around here."

"Rough country's what Geronimo'd be looking for," Vail said thoughtfully.

"That's what's stirring in my mind," Longarm said. "You know, Billy, we can't do much more here to help El Gato, and me and you ain't worked a case together in a coon's age. What if we took a little ride over in the general direction of Tombstone?"

Chapter 13

"That green stretch we're coming to up ahead is about the prettiest thing I've seen since we set out," Vail said. "That country we've just crossed is dryer and hotter than hell and rough as a cob on horses and women."

"All I want to see when we get to them trees ahead is a creek," Longarm told his companion. "If we were to run onto one I couldn't step across without having to stretch my legs, I'd stop and go for a swim."

"It's been a long dry haul," Vail agreed. "Since we left that lake west of where El Gato's set up shop, we haven't seen enough water to make spit in a sandbox."

"If what you're saying is that them hills up ahead look as good to you as they do to me, Billy, I couldn't agree more."

They'd been riding at a deliberate but ground-eating gait while they talked, letting the horses take it easy as the trail started up a long steep grade. The heat haze grew thinner as they ascended the zigzag stretch of trail, and as its distance-distorting shimmer began to vanish they could see low-growing bushes ahead and small trees beyond the brush.

"You ever rub up against Apaches, Billy?" Longarm asked.

"Not the kind that live down here close to Mexico," Vail replied. "About the nearest I got to an Apache was the time I was winding up my stretch in the army. My company was sent to Fort Mohave for a while."

"But that ain't anywhere close to this part of Arizona Territory," Longarm argued. "If I recall, it's way on west and quite a space north, along the Colorado."

"You recall right," Vail admitted. "And there was an Apache town downriver from the fort. Yuman Apaches, they called themselves."

"I don't know all that much about Apaches," Longarm said. "But from what I've heard, there ain't none of 'em that's like human beings."

Vail spoke quickly. "That wasn't what I said. It's Yuman with a *Y*, not human with an *h*. And they didn't give us any trouble, not while I was at Fort Mohave."

"I'll still stand by what I just said, Billy. Maybe you just wasn't at that fort long enough."

"As a matter of fact, I wasn't," Vail told him. "Some jackanapes in the War Department got the idea the fort wasn't worth keeping up, so they closed it down after I'd been there about a month. I heard they opened it up again later, but I had my discharge papers by then."

"You ain't put in much time in Arizona Territory, then?"

"Not more than to travel through it. But I recall sending you out here on a few cases. You ought to know the country."

"Well, I've been around Tombstone a time or two," Longarm replied. "But it was always when I was in a

142

hurry to get someplace else. And I never had a lot to do with redskins when I was here working on a case."

They rode on in silence. In the merciless country across which they had traveled for three days, the heat from the blazing sun made itself felt from an hour or so after sunrise until the same span of time following sunset. Through the hottest part of the day, from midmorning until an hour after dark, its beating rays of molten gold had created a shimmer of heat haze as the barren ground grew warm and the stifling air kept the shimmer until sunset.

Longarm and Vail had quickly formed the habit of stopping in whatever sheltered spot offered itself, and such spots were few indeed. They'd gotten accustomed to keeping their eyes peeled for a place to shelter during the worst of the day. Usually they were able to find a rocky ledge jutting from some tall outcrop where a thin line of shade could be counted on during the day to provide a few hours of relief.

Now, during their fourth day of constant heat, the sight of rising ground and the wooded slopes of low hills ahead was a welcome sight. They reached the greenery after what seemed to be an interminable time and rode on with lifted spirits in the cool breezes that rustled the spiky leaves of the pine and the broader foliage of the aspen trees that now lined the trail.

"I guess this is that last hump El Gato told us to look for," Longarm said as they reined in beside a tinkling shallow creek that had suddenly appeared from nowhere to run beside the trail. He looked around at the half dozen raw, black circles left by the campfires of earlier travelers and said, "Now, if I ain't mistaken, we don't have much more of a ride before we hit Fort Huachuca.

I say we stop here for the night and start early, at first light."

"You won't get any argument from me," Vail told him. "I feel like I've been dragged backwards through a knothole that's a size too small. We've made good time. With an early start and a little luck, we ought to get to Fort Huachuca by noon tomorrow."

"I wish I could tell you men more," the grizzled sergeant at Fort Huachuca told Longarm and Vail. "But all I know is that things are all stirred up. First, every man that could fork a hoss went out looking for Geronimo. Then I got orders over the army telegraph to call in all of them so they'd be here when the new commanding officer shows up. Right now, me and a cook and two hostlers are the only ones here."

"General Crook's being relieved?" Longarm asked.

"He was relieved about a week after Geronimo skedaddled," the sergeant replied. "Relieved and called back to Washington. General Miles is on his way here to take command. That's why all the men are being called back to the fort here. General Miles wants them on hand the minute he pulls in."

Longarm and Vail exchanged brief nods and knowing glances, then Vail asked, "You have any idea when General Miles will be getting here?"

"Sometime before the week's out," the sergeant answered. "He only has to come from Fort Boise."

Before Vail could speak again, Longarm said, "We better come back after he's gotten here, then." He looked at Vail and shook his head almost imperceptibly. "We got some other business to look after while we're waiting."

Vail said nothing, but followed Longarm out of the

headquarters building to the hitch rail. Only after they'd mounted and started toward the road did he turn to Longarm and ask, "I guess this other business you were talking about with the sergeant in there is planning how to go about looking for Geronimo?"

"Why, sure, Billy. Seeing as how I'm still on the Indian Bureau payroll, I've got a duty to earn my keep."

As they rode toward the sally port, Vail asked, "And you think we can find Geronimo, just the two of us, when the army's been beating the bushes for him these past few weeks?"

"Look at it this way, Billy," Longarm said. "Only the good Lord that made this country knows how many gulches and caves and brush patches and hidey-holes there is in it. But I figure the one that'd know next best is Geronimo."

"And you and me, we don't know it at all," Vail said, not even trying to hide his exasperation.

"Now, don't go getting all steamed up," Longarm told him. They were outside the fort's adobe walls now. He pointed toward the single short line of buildings that stood a quarter of a mile away. "We'll likely find a saloon and a store over there, maybe even a rooming house where we can sleep in real beds tonight. And after we've found out a little bit more and looked around a while, then you and me will palaver and see what kind of scheme we can come up with."

"You are quite correct, Marshal Long," General Miles said as he frowned at Longarm across the battered table that served him for a desk. "My orders are to bring Geronimo back here. There aren't any ifs, ands, or buts about it."

"I reckon your folks back in Washington don't know

much about Apaches or about this part of the country, do they?" Longarm asked. He'd gotten over the surprise that he'd had when he first saw the army's most-noted Indian fighter. Miles was a young man, who looked to be in his middle or late thirties.

"Probably not," the general answered. "But the army's gotten a bad name where Indians are concerned."

"I guess that'd be mainly because of Custer?"

"Largely, yes," Miles admitted. "Memories last longer than eight or ten years. People will still remember all the mistakes he made at the Little Big Horn even another ten years from now, perhaps longer. But what's your interest in the Apaches, Marshal Long? As I see it, the army—meaning the man who held the position I have now—made a number of mistakes. I don't intend to repeat them."

"Well, first of all, right now I ain't a U.S. marshal," Longarm said. "But I sorta forgot that when I told your orderly that I needed to talk to you. Right now, I'm doing a kind of special job for the Indian Bureau."

"Which happens to be an outfit for which I have very little respect," Miles snapped.

"I figured that might be the case," Longarm said. "But that's not here nor there. What you're after is getting Geronimo and his Apaches back from Mexico without a lot of fuss, muss, and bother. Am I right, General?"

"I suppose you could put it that way," Miles agreed after a moment of thoughtful silence. "Always supposing that they're in Mexico. It's been quite a while since they got away, you know, and they could be almost anywhere by now."

"Oh, I figure you're right about 'em being on the

other side of the border," Longarm admitted. "You've fought the redskins enought to know something about 'em."

"Yes, I suppose you could say that," Miles agreed. "The Comanches and Kiowas in Texas and the Sioux in Montana and the Nez Perces in Idaho. And if you don't mind me pointing it out, I've managed to win when the chips were down."

"But you've never run up against the Apaches," Longarm said, his voice carefully expressionless.

"Not until now."

"They ain't like them other Indians you've fought before, you know."

"An ounce of lead in the right place makes every Indian equal," Miles said.

"And I don't guess you ever had a run-in with the Mexican rurales, either?"

"What's that got to do with it? I've heard of them, of course, and they're little more than a crooked police force."

Longarm shook his head. "They're a lot closer to Apaches than they are to any police force you'd ever be likely to find."

"I still don't see what you're driving at," Miles objected.

Reaching into his pocket, Longarm took out the letter sent to the rurales by their commanding officer. He asked, "I don't reckon you know the Mexican lingo, do you, General?"

"No. I've never been on Mexican border service before."

"But you know a little bit about the rurales, I guess?" Longarm went on.

"Every military man does, I'm sure. They're just an

example of a good fighting force gone wrong."

"Wrong or right, if you take your men into Mexico, you're going to meet up with 'em, General. They'll be ready to start the shooting, and they won't wait for you to begin."

"You'd better explain how you can be sure of that, Long."

"This piece of paper I got here is orders from the head of the rurales to his men. It tells 'em to give Geronimo anything he wants: ammunition, grub, whatever. And it also tells 'em not to let you or any of your men go across the border. If it comes to a shooting showdown, they got orders to shoot."

"Why, that amounts to a declaration of war!" Miles gasped.

"It wouldn't be the first war we've had with Mexico, but I guess you know that."

"Quite well. So does the secretary of war. I don't know whether you're aware of it, Long, but the army has standing orders that we're never to provoke any border incidents with Mexico."

"I don't know all that much about the army, but it stands to reason," Longarm commented. "I don't guess you'd mind having Geronimo handed over to you?"

"My orders are to get Geronimo and his Apaches and transport them to the reservation that's being fixed for them in Florida," Miles said. "How I go about doing that is up to me. Suppose you tell me what you have in mind."

"Well, we got two weeks, Billy," Longarm told Vail. "I got to admit, we got a real job cut out for us to hand

Geronimo over to General Miles by then, even if we can find him."

"I still think it's a harebrained scheme," Vail said. "But I've put up with you so far, so I guess we'll keep on going. And I don't mind telling you, I'm enjoying all this a hell of a lot more than I do riding herd on a desk in Denver."

"Sure," Longarm said. "Now let's push on. We still got a ways to go before we hit the border, then we'll have to see what kind of luck we have keeping on Geronimo's trail."

Ahead of them, the rising sun cast long shadows from even the smallest stones or clods of earth that broke the surface of the barren land. Since leaving Fort Huachuca, they'd been riding in a series of sweeping zigzags across the desert that stretched endlessly before them, trying to pick up a trail that was already far too old.

It was an unfriendly land over which they were riding. Here and there the tall spindly stems of the yucca rose from the grey-green leaves that curved from the yellow soil. Rocks surfaced in unexpected places, their edges rising from the baked earth and running for short distances to form jagged ledges before vanishing beneath the soil again. Clumps of earth, the marks left by coyotes or panthers digging for a rabbit or a gopher, cast shadows that blotted the yellowish crust of soil for a yard or two.

At this early hour of the morning the country was even more deserted than it was during the hours of darkness. Its regular inhabitants had gone to bed, for they had learned to hunt by night. Except for the little johnny owls that lived in burrows or found shelter in rock crevices, only the birds lived and hunted by day, and they were just beginning to come out. It was the circling of buzzards a mile or so away that drew Longarm's attention first.

"They got something on the ground over there," he told Vail, pointing to the black silhouettes against the brightening sky. "If there wasn't but one buzzard, I wouldn't pay 'im no mind, it'd just be what's left of a rabbit or coyote. But this is big enough to keep four or five of them buzzards busy. We better go take a look-see."

Reining toward the circling scavengers, they moved toward them. As they drew closer, Longarm and Vail could watch the bird war that was taking place as the buzzards fought with each other for a chance at whatever kind of food was attracting them. When they were still closer, Longarm and Vail exchanged quick glances, for now they could see that the elongated form which was the objective of the soaring birds was—or had been—human.

"Likely a desert rat looking for gold where there ain't none now nor ever was," Longarm said.

"We'd better make sure," Vail replied.

"Oh, no two ways about that, Billy."

In another few minutes they were close enough to alarm the scavenging birds. There were a half dozen of them, and all but two made the short, ungainly run that was needed to get off the ground as the two riders drew nearer. Then the last pair took flight and joined the four which had left earlier. They did not go far, but began flying in a wider loop. They were obviously watching and waiting, and both Longarm and Vail got the eerie feeling that comes to any human being regarded as a meal for a wild creature.

"Those damn buzzards make me nervous," Vail growled.

"You ain't got a thing to worry about, Billy," Longarm assured him. "As long as we're able to move, that is."

"I know," Vail grunted. "I've seen buzzards before now, Long. But just the same, they get me edgy when I look at them."

Longarm did not answer; he'd reined in and was bending over the body that lay sprawled on the earth. Although the scavengers had been busy, it was obvious that their work had begun only a short time earlier, for there were still long shreds of flesh clinging to the corpse's bones.

"He was Apache, all right," Longarm said as Vail dismounted and came up to the skeletal form. "And he ain't been laying here too long. Look."

He pointed to the skull, the face now stripped to a few strings of sinew. However, the buzzards had not yet town away all the flesh. A band of cloth still circled the skeletal form's skull and kept in place a shock of ink-black hair that fanned out above the corpse's shoulder bones. Almost hidden by the rib cage, a tattered leather pouch that obviously had been worked on by animal claws showed glints of yellow metal in several slashes.

"He was Apache, all right. And you can tell from that pouch that he must've had a gun. But if he did, where'd it get off to?" Vail frowned. "And where's his horse?"

"Now, that's a good question," Longarm replied. "But I got a hunch we might find an answer or two if we do some backtracking. There's only one place I figure this fellow could've come from, Billy. That's the place where Geronimo and the rest of them Apaches has holed up. And once we find that place—well, that's all she wrote."

Chapter 14

"Are you serious, Long?" Vail asked. "How do you figure that this might be one of the Apaches that was with Geronimo?"

"Because of what General Miles told us. If you recall, he said Geronimo's bunch didn't have enough guns to go around."

"I recall him saying that, but I still don't follow you," Vail complained.

Longarm pointed to the pouch with its metal glints picking up the rays of the sun. "Whoever this fellow was, he had a rifle, and maybe a pistol, too. But there ain't no sign of 'em now, and I don't see a knife or war club, either."

"Why, the answer to that's easy to come by," Vail said. "If he had a rifle, somebody took it."

"Oh, I figured that right off, Billy. But don't forget, whoever this fellow was, he was bound to be an Apache."

"Sure"—Vail nodded—"that headband's a give-away."

"So is there not being a gun or knife anyplace around."

"Just how do you figure that?"

"One thing I know about Apaches is that when one of the men dies in a fight they don't leave him lay," Longarm explained. "If they can, they carry him to his house. And they don't take his gun or knife or club away. They put 'em alongside of him and set fire to the house. They believe that'll get his weapons and his soul or spirit into their heaven at the same time."

Vail shook his head. "It beats all what some people believe in, doesn't it?"

"My bet is that Geronimo's short of guns," Longarm went on, as though Vail hadn't spoken. "Knives, too, I'd imagine. So even if it went against their religion, they took his along."

"So, that's why this fellow didn't have either a gun of a knife." Vail nodded.

"Either that, or Geronimo figured that the live Apaches had more use for 'em than the dead one," Longarm said. "Except that if there'd been other Apaches with him when he died, they'd've laid him out proper, with his head to the sunrise and face covered up."

"What in hell would he've been doing here by himself?" Vail asked.

"Maybe he'd got his bellyful of running with Geronimo and he was going back to Fort Huachuca to give up. If Geronimo was to let any of his men do that, he'd lose face. So Geronimo shot him and left him laying here, but took his gun and knife because they needed 'em real bad."

"I'd imagine your guess is better than mine, Long," Vail said thoughtfully. "You're bound to've picked up a

154

lot of things about how Indians figure, as many cases as you've been on over in the Indian Nation."

"I ain't sure that helps much. Apaches are a cut apart from all the other tribes. They're outlaw Indians. Now, I got a hunch that if we backtrack this fellow here we got a pretty good chance of running across Geronimo's trail someplace not too far up ahead."

"You don't figure he'll have hidden his trail?"

"I figure he was in too big a hurry to put some miles between him and the fort to bother with that."

"You might just be right," Vail admitted.

"All we can do is try," Longarm said.

"Luck's been with us so far. Maybe it'll hold out." Vail surveyed the expanse of bare, featureless baked earth surrounding them, the tracks made by the moccasins of the dead Apache barely visible, and asked, "Suppose we run out of tracks to follow?"

"About the best thing I can come up with if that happens is for us to lay down a snake trail," Longarm replied.

"Fine. Now if you'll just tell me what that means we can get started," Vail said.

"It ain't all that hard, Billy. But it's easier to show than tell." Hunkering down, he scratched a wide shallow vee in the yellow soil. Looking up at Vail, he said, "One of us goes like this." As he spoke he was drawing a similar vee that slanted away from the first and connected with its points, forming a diamond. "The other one goes like this," he went on. "Except we don't quite come together. This way we'll be covering the most ground in the quickest time."

Vail nodded. "I follow you. Those sides look sorta like the trail a snake leaves when it's wiggling along."

"Now you got the idea," Longarm said. "We slant

out till we're just about to lose sight of each other, then we begin slanting back till we almost come together."

"Fine," Vail said. "And on horseback we'll be covering the ground a lot faster than that redskin could walking."

Swinging into their saddles, they started out, riding side by side. Both men kept their eyes on the ground. Even though being on horseback raised their eyes very little higher above the desert soil than would have been the case had they been walking, the faint scuff marks left by the dead Apache's moccasins were clearly visible where the sand was soft and deep. In places where the surface had crusted over, the footprints vanished for a short distance now and again, but soon reappeared.

For the first few miles they were able to keep their horses at a steady walk, then they entered an area where boulders rose in countless numbers and the surface was more stone than soil. After they'd ridden fifteen or twenty yards over the treacherous, unyielding stone, Longarm reined in.

"We sure ain't going to find much along here where the ground's too hard to hold tracks," he said. "Let's push across this mean spot fast as we can, Billy. It ought not stretch too far. Chances are we'll pick up Geronimo's trail on the other side of this stretch of rock."

Moving gingerly of necessity, Longarm and Vail coaxed their horses across the stone carpace. Now and then the iron-shod hooves of one of the animals slipped, but the horses always managed to recover their precarious footing. They reached the end of the treacherous stretch of solid stone and reined in. For a moment they rested in their saddles, surveying the terrain ahead.

Between them and the horizon nothing moved. The gently rolling surface of tan-hued sandy soil showed no tracks, and an occasional clump of ocotilla cactus or the spindly stalk of a yucca plant was the only vegetation in sight.

"Maybe this'd be the place for us to split up and try that snake trail you were telling me about," Vail suggested.

"It's sure the best way to cover a lot of ground without wasting much time," Longarm agreed. He swept his hand wide to encompass the vast deserted stretch of featureless terrain. "If there's any tracks out there, we'll have to be right on top of 'em before we can see 'em."

"Let's get started, then." Vail nodded and kicked his horse into motion. "I'll go right, you go left."

Longarm started moving as Vail rode away on a long slant. He watched Vail for a moment, fixing in his mind the direction he was taking, then scanned the barren terrain in the opposite direction, seeking a landmark by which he could guide himself. A lone yucca, its thin stalk broken in the center, was the only point of reference that he found. Longarm toed the animal ahead and started riding slowly, his eyes on the barren sandy soil.

Riding a straight line was more difficult than Longarm had thought it would be. Time after time the horse would begin veering slowly, almost imperceptibly, first to one side, then to the other, and Longarm was forced to twitch the reins to put it back on the imaginary line he was following. Now and then he glanced at Vail, distant from him now, but still a long way from being out of sight below the horizon.

Though he kept his eyes on the ground ahead as he rode, Longarm saw no signs that anyone had passed that way recently enough for either the hoofprints of a horse or the impression of a sandaled foot to have survived the gentle intermittent desert breeze. He'd almost reached

157

the broken yucca now, and glanced once more across the wide expanse of desert.

When his eyes reached Vail his interest perked up at once, for it was plain that his companion had found something. Vail was standing up in his stirrups, clinging to the reins of his horse with one hand, while with the other hand he was waving his hat to draw Longarm's attention.

Longarm waved in reply, and Vail began swinging one arm, a signal that he'd found something. Longarm wheeled his mount and started across the hard sand, riding in a straight line to join Vail.

"There were some Indians fighting here not too long ago," Vail told Longarm as he reined in. He gestured toward some bits of shining copper and a few charred scraps of cloth that lay on the baked ground a few feet from them. "Caps and scraps of wadding. Take a look for yourself."

Longarm dismounted and bent down to examine the debris. There was not enough to hold his attention for more than a moment or two. The scattered bits of cloth and metal stood out in sharp contrast against the barren ground. Bending closer to one of the bits of cloth, Longarm could see that its edges were charred and black. Then he examined the bits of copper. All of them were rounded in small arcs and showed sharply serrated fracture lines.

"Billy, do you make these little bits and pieces out the same as I do?" he asked Vail as he straightened up.

"Wadding and caps," Vail replied. "I've seen the like many a time. I learned to shoot with a muzzle loader."

"That's what they're out of, all right." Longarm nodded. "And nobody much shoots a muzzle loader anymore. Nobody except redskins, that is."

"I figure it's where Geronimo and the Apaches had a fight with somebody," Vail went on. "And just lately, too."

"Oh, sure. Them little scraps of wadding ain't had time to scatter, and the copper's still bright. But if there was a fight here, there oughta be more of 'em laying around."

"That's what occurred to me, too, Long. But it wouldn't take very much of a breeze to scatter those little bits of cloth to hell and gone."

"I guess you scouted around a little ways while I was getting over here?" Longarm asked.

"Sure. As soon as I was sure you got my signal. I looked all over, but I didn't want to go too far away. I didn't find anything else."

"Ground's too hard," Longarm noted. "There's soft spots every now and then, though. I reckon it'd be a right smart idea for us to mount up and look around a little bit."

Old hands that they were in such matters, Longarm and Vail had no need to talk things over. Longarm nodded toward the south and then touched his chest with his forefinger as he brought it around to the west. Vail nodded and started for his horse. They were moving within less than a minute after agreeing on their next move.

Longarm had traveled only a few hundred feet, riding in a zigzag pattern, when he came to a high formation of jagged, wind-eroded sandstone that jutted up abruptly, like an array of miniature turrets, from the otherwise unbroken level ground. He'd noticed the outcrop before, but had given it no real thought, for such formations were common enough in that area. Around this one, though, the hard ground had a look that was not quite right. Somehow it differed from the surface soil a few feet farther away from the outcrop's base. He reined his horse over to examine it more closely.

Even before he'd dismounted, he saw the reason for the difference. Around the base of the upthrust, ocher-colored rock, the ground had been beaten smoother than the surrounding soil by the trampling of many feet. Swinging from his saddle, Longarm walked up to the short, rough-surfaced columns of pinkish red rock and stood examining it for a moment.

A half dozen rounded sandstone columns, jagged-surfaced and striated, made up the formation. All but one of them presented the same appearance. In the one that had drawn his eye, two of the wriggling vertical striations were darker, deeper, and much more pronounced than was the case with the others.

Leaning forward, Longarm took hold of the column and shook it. The stubby spire split and a section of it toppled outward. Having the section of stone separate was such a surprise that, even though Longarm moved with his usual quickness, the long loose piece of stone almost knocked him down before he could brace his feet to grasp it and let it fall forward easily.

He eased the loose, unwieldy chunk of sandstone to the ground and released it. Then he stared at the cavity that the section of rock had concealed and his jaw dropped. In the bottom of the long, narrow cavity, impressed in the thin layers of desert sand that had blown in through the slits between the crevices, there were two narrow oval indentations. What had made them was obvious even at a glance; it was not even necessary for Longarm to lean forward to examine them more closely. The impressions could only have been made by the buttstocks of two rifles.

"Well, old son," Longarm muttered, "it looks like

you've found a cache where somebody had a couple of rifles stashed away. And it's certain-sure that the kind of hidey-hole them guns was in likely wasn't made by nobody but Geronimo. He's the only one that's smart enough to hide guns this way, just in case he might need 'em sometime. So that means him and his men's got at least them two rifles now."

Stepping away from the formation, Longarm looked for Billy Vail. He saw him almost at once, a good three quarters of a mile distant. His back was toward Longarm. The distance was too great for a shout to carry. Longarm was forced to stand and wait patiently until Vail turned to look back. Then Longarm lifted his arm and swung his forearm several times. Vail turned his mount and started back at a fast canter. There was little now that Longarm could do but wait. He lighted a cigar and hunkered down in the sparse shade provided by the rock formation and puffed his cheroot thoughtfully while he watched Vail approaching. He'd consumed an inch or more of the long thin cigar when Vail reined in beside him.

"I take it you've run onto something?" he asked.

"We got a place here to start trailing from," Longarm told him. He gestured toward the rock formation and said, "There was a couple of rifles stashed away in that tall rock. Couldn't have been nobody but Geronimo that'd think about a trick like that. So we've picked up his trail, if he's left one we're smart enough to follow."

While Longarm was talking, Vail stepped over to the rock outcrop. He peered into the hollowed stone and leaned forward to stick his hand inside. He was dragging his fingers through the thick layer of sandy dust in the bottom when they encountered something hard. He fingered it for a moment before realizing what it was.

161

Then he held it out for Longarm to inspect.

"If this belonged to those guns, we're not going to have to worry a lot when we catch up to Geronimo. Look here."

Longarm looked at the tiny copper cylinder, age-corroded to a deep reddish hue. "I'll be damned!" he exclaimed. "If it ain't a percussion cap! Why, they ain't used caps on rifles for twenty years or more! There ain't nobody but redskins that'd have a gun like that!"

"Then it's got to be one Geronimo hid away out here," Vail observed. "When you stop to think about it, his idea makes a lot of sense, Long. Haven't there been times when you could've used a gun that you'd hidden away against the day you might need it?"

"More'n a time or two," Longarm admitted. "You got to give that Geronimo credit. He's one cagey Indian! It wasn't nothing but bull luck that I found this stash of his."

"Well, at least we know we're on his trail," Vail said. "I guess the best thing for us to do now is see if we can follow it fast enough to catch up with him."

"If we circle this rock and widen out from it as we go, we're bound to find it," Longarm said. "Let's go after it!"

Mounting, Longarm and Vail began casting increasingly wider circles around the stone formation that had given them their clue. They rode unhurriedly, taking their time in examining the hard-baked crust of the coarse, dry desert soil. Even so, the morning was well along before they came to an area where crusted soil gave way to shifting sand. There, at last, they saw the mingled prints of an uncountable number of moccasin-clad feet leading in a line that ran as straight as a taut string across the desert. During the time that had passed since the tracks were made, the wind had already begun to fill and level out the depressions.

"That's got to be Geronimo and his bunch!" Vail exclaimed.

"Sure," Longarm said. "And it's a shame we didn't get here when them tracks were fresh. Can you make out how many there are with him, Billy?"

After studying the marked path Vail shook his head. "No. There might be any number, from ten or a dozen to maybe thirty."

"That's what I read, too," Longarm agreed. "But now that we've found these tracks, let's push on fast as we can. With any luck and a little bit of sense, we'll get that slippery Apache before he's too deep into Mexico."

Chapter 15

"If we don't run across a water hole pretty soon, these nags are going to be in right bad shape," Vail said to Longarm as they reined in at the drop-off of a steep ledge and looked at the barren landscape that unfolded below them.

Longarm nodded without speaking. He knew Vail realized that both of them were aware of the strain they'd been putting on the horses since starting from the gun cache in the rock formation.

It had been a hard ride. An hour or more before noon the sun's rays had gotten even hotter than usual, and the blazing orb had grown progressively hotter after it passed its zenith and started its slow descent. Both the men and their horses were affected by the increased heat. To save the animals' flagging strength, Longarm and Vail had moved more and more slowly, letting their mounts set their own pace.

They'd made slow progress in the last few hours. They were now fighting both nature and the skill Geronimo showed in hiding the traces of his Apache band.

The trail at times was almost invisible, especially where nature seemed to be one of the most valuable allies the Apaches had. There were long stretches where sand gave way to hard-baked, dark-brown loam on which the sandals of the fleeing Indians left virtually no traces. Now, with the sun slowly declining, the effects of its heat on the air seemed to be magnified. Instead of a thin, transparent shimmer, it had become an almost translucent wall that veiled the distance and the lower part of the vast arc of copper sky.

With the heat increasing as the blazing sun continued its slow descent in the west, the film of heat haze filled the air almost as thickly as a fog. The shimmer of its haze distorted distances, and the few dull, green clumps of cactus and yucca showed only as blurs through the veil of golden heat.

"I've been watching ahead as best I can," Longarm said as they turned to follow the rim of the ledge where they'd made their brief stop. "Unless I'm seeing something I just think I'd like to be looking at, we might find some water after we get down off this ledge."

"You're seeing more than I can, then," Vail said. "Show me and let's find out if what you think you see is real."

Narrowing his eyes to slits, Longarm peered along the desert terrain where it stretched away from the bottom of the bluff. It took a moment for him to relocate the hint of green that he'd been almost sure he'd seen a moment earlier.

"There it is," he said, pointing to what at first glance seemed to be only a small distortion in the translucent air.

Vail studied the spot for a moment, then he nodded and replied, "I believe you're right, Long. Maybe we'd better head for it, even if it means leaving the trail we're on. We can always come back here and pick it up, but my bet's that we don't need to worry too much. If there's water in that place, it's a sure bet that Geronimo and his bunch headed for it, just like we're doing."

"First thing we got to do is find a place to get down this damn bluff without killing our horses," Longarm pointed out. "A busted leg'd stop us dead."

They moved ahead, but with more caution now. Though they continued to scan the narrow trail for tracks, hoofprints, or moccasin scuffs, the thin sandy soil had begun to give way to porous lava rock. The rock had surfaced at intervals earlier in small outcrops that showed dark reddish brown under a thin cover of yellowish sand. It appeared first as granules, then the granules increased to thumb-sized pieces, and now as the thumb-sized pieces merged with porous flat-sized chunks, there was no way of telling whether or not the trail had been used lately, no clues or even hints as to who—if anyone—had passed that way before.

Several minutes passed before they came to a break in the ledge from which a jagged swath of disturbed earth led to the slope at its base. Longarm and Vail did not need to consult about their next move. Longarm was riding at the rim of the drop-off a bit ahead of Vail. He reined his horse into the break and the animal hunkered down its haunches and began a descent that was about equally divided between walking, sliding, and floundering down the stony vestigial path.

Both men reached the bottom without harm to themselves or their horses. They let their panting mounts stand until their sides stopped heaving, then turned them in the direction where they'd seen the hint of green. In spite of their urgency to press on to the shred of greenery that promised water, Longarm and Vail did not push their horses even now. They still allowed the animals to set their own pace along the base of the steep, striated rise.

Although the slow rate of progress they were forced to maintain on the treacherous slipping rocks made the distance to the still-visible shred of green seem greater than it was, they finally reached their objective. A yawning gap appeared in the towering wall along which they were riding. The horses were raising their heads and plodding a bit faster now, showing a new eagerness to move ahead.

"Dollars to doughnuts there's water just inside that gap," Longarm commented. "The nags can smell it from where we are now, even if we can't."

"It seems to me like they're perking up a bit," Vail said. "And I could stand a little perking up myself. That damn sun's hot enough to fry a man's brains, even if he hasn't taken off his hat."

They reached the streak of green that had first drawn their attention. It was a straggle of scrub cedar, tiny trees no higher than a man's knees, with short, thumb-sized trunks and branches no bigger in diameter than matchsticks, clinging to the edges of a wide opening that cut in a narrow vee down the slanting face of the brownish red rock.

Longarm reined in and Vail pulled his horse up beside him. For a moment they sat in silence, examining the fist-sized rocks that stretched ahead of the horses' hooves into the yawning split in the high wall of the extinct volcano that towered above their heads.

"So far we ain't seen a smidgen of a sign on this trail that there's been anybody along it for a coon's age," Longarm said.

"Maybe there hasn't," Vail suggested. "For all we can be sure of, we might've wandered off that little trace of trail we started following. It'd be easy to do in country like this."

"I guess I better go take a look-see in there before we ride in," Longarm told his companion. "I'd a lot sooner be thirsty than fall into a trap, and this place looks like it could sure turn into one."

"It's the kind of place Geronimo'd be likely to know about," Vail agreed.

"That's why I figure to look before we jump."

"Suppose we both go in," Vail said. He waved his hand to take in the desert that stretched away below them. "There's sure no way anybody can get here across that without us seeing them. And I don't see any trail leading here."

"Chances are we wouldn't. That stretch we just came over was harder than a lot of rocks," Longarm replied. "But that ain't what I had in mind."

"I know what you've got on your mind," Vail said. "This is the only place we've run across so far that'd make a good hideout, and just as sure as God made little green apples, we're not the first ones to run into it."

"Something like that," Longarm agreed. "But we ain't going to get no place just sitting out here yattering. Let's copper our bets, though, Billy. We'll leave the horses out here, in case we get into something real bad when we go into that cut."

"Fair enough," Vail agreed.

Longarm was already dismounting and Vail moved quickly to swing off his own horse. Tethering the animals to the sturdiest scrub cedar they could find, both men slid their rifles from their saddle scabbards and started in through the yawning gap that ran down the jagged side of the extinct volcano.

Under their boot soles the porous lava rock grated loudly as they moved along the narrow passage that ran string-straight through the wide slit. The passageway was dim compared to the blazing sunlight to which they'd been exposed on the slope outside. It was also surprisingly long, extending for fifty or sixty yards between bare towering walls that cut out the sunlight and left its entire length in deep shadow.

Longarm and Vail advanced steadily but cautiously, their boot soles grating on the loose shifting rock underfoot. Through the V-shaped gap that opened into the long-dead crater they could see the opposite wall of the interior, and it seemed a long distance away.

To their surprise, they could also see the last thing they expected: the shining thread of a little stream that gushed from the far wall of the crater and splashed in a jagged shallow channel down its rugged sides.

"You know, Billy, I got more'n just a little hunch that we might find Geronimo and his bunch inside there," Longarm said to his companion. "If anybody'd know about this place, it'd sure be the Apaches."

"If they do happen to be holed up in there, we've sure got 'em in a bottle," Vail replied.

"Sure," Longarm agreed. "But the trouble is, if they are in there, we'll have to be the cork that keeps the bottle closed."

"Narrow as this gap is, we ought not have too much trouble doing that."

"We won't. Not as long as our ammunition holds out. But let's not waste good time on maybes and ifs. I don't see nothing stirring out there in that hole, but we

170

ain't going to know for sure till we get to the end of this gap."

Almost before Longarm had finished speaking the end of the passageway loomed in front of them. They did not need to speak or plan. Each of them knew that the other could be trusted to react quickly and correctly in any situation that might develop.

Vail stepped to the left side of the wide opening, Longarm to the right. They advanced to the edge of the passage and stopped. Longarm pushed his wide-brimmed hat back on his head until it fell to hang between his shoulders by its chin strap. He gripped his rifle by the forestock in his left hand. He could either raise the rifle and bring it to bear on a target in a split second, or could sweep his Colt from its holster and fire in even less time than would be required to aim and trigger the rifle. Moving as close as he could to the end of the passage, he peered out into the dead volcano's crater.

Although the sun had already started down in the west and the bottom of the crater was in shade, the sub-dued light at its floor was still bright, and for a moment Longarm did not quite believe his eyes. The interior of the crater covered almost as much space as the central square of a small town. The water from the creek that splashed in its cascading arc from the wall of the volcanic crater ran down its jagged side in a small but bois-terous channel to form a pond near the center of the crater's floor.

More startling than the pool were the several small buildings that Longarm saw. None of them stood near the center of the spacious bottom, but were all close by its slanting walls. Most of them had been built with weathered boards, their walls leaning slightly off plumb, their doors swinging open, their windows glassless. The remaining huts were constructed of crumbling cornered adobe bricks.

Still more surprising than either the pool of water or the buildings was the handful of rurales who were lounging beside the pool. Three of them were hunkered down around a serape that had been spread on the ground. They were playing cards while the remaining two looked on. All of them wore the ornate gold-embroidered sombreros, high-crowned with wide, up-curling brims, and the dark suits of charro jackets and trousers with wide, flared bottoms and ruffled triangular inserts above the cuffs that through the years had become the unofficial uniform of the band.

"What's got you stopped there, Long?" Billy Vail whispered from behind Longarm.

Longarm moved back beside Vail before he replied, "Plumb damn surprise, Billy. You wouldn't believe it if I told you, so I guess you better look for yourself. Step up and peek, but do it real careful."

Vail stepped up to the spot Longarm had occupied. He gazed around the edge of the cut for several moments, then stepped back. Longarm had moved another step or two back into the cut, and Vail joined him.

"What in hell are those rurales doing here?" he asked. "They're not supposed to cross the border any more than one of us is supposed to go into Mexico unless we're chasing a man we're after!"

"Oh, I know that," Longarm answered. "But for all you or me knows, it's us that's on the wrong side of the border now."

"I guess it's possible," Vail said thoughtfully. "But I won't believe it until I see a survey line."

"Which you ain't likely to do. But I got the same

feeling you have, Billy. I don't believe we covered enough ground today to be in Mexico."

"Why, hell!" Vail went on. "They've got a regular little settlement in there! And we don't have any idea how many more there are in those shanties."

"So we don't," Longarm agreed. "And we're not after any rurales, all we want is Geronimo and his outlaw Apaches."

"I sure didn't see any Apaches hanging around in there," Vail said.

"No. But that don't mean they ain't holed up in there. We didn't take time to look a lot."

"Even if we had, we couldn't've seen all of that hole," Vail said, a frown taking shape on his sober face. "Those walls inside there curve around pretty sharp."

"How many rurales would you say there are, Billy? We only saw five."

"Well, there's a half-dozen shacks, and it wouldn't surprise me to find a cave or two in the walls in there," Vail said.

"I didn't see any horses, either," Longarm went on. "And I've never yet run into a rurale that'd walk anyplace."

"They'll have horses, for sure, and since we haven't seen any, they're bound to be in the part of that hole we can't see from here."

"We might find that we've run into a whole damned company of rurales if we started stirring things up," Longarm suggested.

"We might. But I've never known you to let a little thing like that stop you."

"Oh, it ain't going to stop me, Billy. We've got the best answer in the world to them rurales in that holster hanging behind my saddle outside."

"I'd completely forgotten about it!" Vail exclaimed. "But you're right! With my Winchester and Colt and that nonstop shooter of yours, we ought to be able to take the rurales no matter how many there are!"

"If you'll just stand watch by yourself a minute, I'll step outside and fetch it."

Without waiting for Vail to reply, Longarm started for the outside opening of the slit. He returned in a few moments carrying the bag in which he'd nursed Theo Bryson's invention since leaving Denver. He opened the bag, and Vail leaned forward to watch while Longarm assembled the gun, fitting the long magazine to the grip. Then he pulled back the loading lever to feed the first shell into the chamber and hefted the clumsy weapon experimentally.

"Looks like I'm all set," he announced. "Do you figure we oughta give them rurales a chance to give up, before I start shooting?"

"I don't imagine they'd feel obliged to give you a chance; you know what the rurales are like," Vail replied. "But if it'll make you feel better, tell 'em they can give up before you start shooting. You're the one on the firing line, but I'd sure argue with you for the job if I knew how to handle that damn gun."

"Well, now," Longarm replied, "that saves us fussing, don't it?" He found the balance point he'd been trying to locate and cradled the clumsy-looking repeater in his hands. Then he said, "I guess I'm as ready as I'll ever be."

Holding Theo's invention as though he'd been shooting with it all his life, Longarm stepped outside the passageway.

Chapter 16

For a full minute the rurales who were gambling beside the pool were so engrossed in their game that they paid no attention to Longarm. Then one of them glanced up and saw him. Waving his hand in a friendly greeting, the rurale called, *"Hola, amigo! Que pasa por—"* Then he realized belatedly that Longarm was a stranger, not one of the rurales. His voice changed instantly from a tone of friendliness to a shout of alarm as he shouted, *"Extranjero! Tomemos instantaneamente!"*

Even before the gambling rurale sounded the alarm, those who'd been watching the game were reaching for their holstered pistols. Longarm had no real choice. He swung the muzzle of the rapid-fire gun and touched the trigger.

Though Longarm's finger pressed the trigger for only a second or less, a stream of bullets spurted from his weapon. The rurales who'd been standing beside the gamblers reeled and dropped as the slugs tore into them. In Longarm's hands the rapid-fire gun was bucking, trying to pull itself out of his grip.

As he fought the weapon, trying to control it, Longarm depressed the muzzle slightly. The stream of hot lead pouring from the weapon swept across the three rurales hunkered down by the serape. They were in an unhandy position to draw, and all of them started to get to their feet. Before they could straighten up, the stream of lead caught them and they collapsed beside their fellows.

Only a minute or two had passed since the first staccato of shots broke the silence of the volcano's crater, and two rurales were emerging from one of the huts. Vail caught sight of them and swung his rifle. He fired and one of them dropped. The other rurale was carrying a rifle. He started to bring it up, swinging it toward the group near the entry. Vail brought the rurale down with his next shot.

Longarm had succeeded in controlling the weapon by this time. He looked from one of the shanties to another, seeking a target, and found one when two more rurales, hatless and carrying pistols in their hands, ran out of one of the adobe buildings.

Before they could raise their pistols, Longarm brought up the muzzle of his deadly weapon and touched the trigger. He'd learned from his first shots and depressed it for only a moment. The gun chattered in a quick burst. Bullets kicked spurts of dust from the building's walls as Longarm fanned his fire across the front. Then the deadly stream of lead reached the men who were bringing up their own guns. They spun around as the slugs from the gun caught them, and without either of the pair having gotten off a shot they dropped beside the building wall.

Men were running from all the huts now. Some came rushing from the doors carrying rifles or pistols, but a few were empty-handed. Vail's Winchester cracked again and one of the onrushing rurales broke stride, stumbled, and pitched forward on his face. When he was sure the rurale would not get up, Vail sought another target.

Longarm had already found one. Three men came out of one of the larger huts and he started swinging the rapid-fire gun in their direction. Before he could trigger the weapon one of the trio pulled a white handkerchief from his pocket and began waving it frantically.

"Rendimos!" he shouted. *"Rendimos instantamente! No tirate mas! Luchamos instantamente!"*

Longarm glanced around the interior of the crater. Wherever he saw a rurale, the man was standing still with his arms raised as high as possible.

Glancing at Vail, he asked, "You figure we can trust 'em?"

"If I ever saw a beat bunch, this is it," Vail replied. "I guess that fellow that yelled at us to stop shooting is their boss, and it sure seems like they've had a bellyful."

Nodding, Longarm turned his attention back to the rurale who'd given the cease-fire command. Stepping forward, he called, "Are you the boss of this bunch?"

"I am *commandante, sí,*" the rurale replied.

"Then tell them men to put their guns down and move out in the open, by that puddle of water," Longarm went on. "We're going to be watching, and we'll shoot the first one that makes any kind of wrong move!"

"Sí, sí!" the rurale replied. Then he shouted, *"Ponganse sus fusiles! No combatemos mas! Tenemos paz! Concursen a la fuente inmediamente!"*

Longarm and Vail stepped into the open now. They held their weapons ready and kept their eyes shifting over the crater while the rurales moved slowly toward the pool.

Once they'd gotten all the way inside the crater, they could see for the first time that it was larger than they'd thought. The walls of the big circular opening rose high, and on them rough paths had been hewed in the porous rock. The paths led to a half dozen or more buildings that had been built at three levels above the bottom, and men were filing along each one, heading for the pool.

"Looks like we got a whole damn passel of rurales here," Longarm said to Vail in a half whisper. "Now we got to figure out what we can do with 'em!"

"We'll come up with something," Vail said. "But there's one thing that bothers me, Long. We're not sure whether we're still in the United States of whether we've crossed the border into Mexico. If we've done that, then the rurales are on their own home grounds."

"I don't know any more about that than you do," Longarm replied. "But I'm willing to gamble we're still on the safe side of the border. If we wasn't, that officer wouldn't've been so quick to give up, even if we did have him in a bind."

"You might just be right," Vail replied. His voice was thoughtful. "If we're in Mexico, he'd have put up more of a fight."

"I'd say we hold the high cards right now," Longarm went on. "Let's get him over here and see what he's got to say."

Turning back to face the assembling rurales, Longarm scanned the group until he located the one who'd ordered the cease-fire. He caught the rurale's eye and beckoned for him to come join him and Vail. The man moved slowly and his face showed his reluctance, but he obeyed Longarm's gesture. Weaving his way through the shifting, chattering group of his men, he came to where Longarm and Vail were standing. He said nothing, but looked from one of them to the other, his eyes questioning.

"I guess you speak English," Longarm began. "Because you sure did savvy what I said to you a while ago."

"I espeak a leetle, *sí*," the rurale replied.

"My name's Long," Longarm went on. "Custis Long, deputy United States marshal on temporary service with the Indian Bureau. This here's Billy Vail, he's a chief deputy U.S. marshal outa Denver."

While the rurale did not offer to shake hands, he bobbed his head in a half bow and replied, "I am Leon Mercado, *lugarteniente de rurales*."

"Me and Billy is chasing after a redskin prisoner and his bunch that got away from Fort Huachuca. I reckon you know it's just a little ways north of here," Longarm said.

"*Por cierto, señor*," the rurale replied.

"And since you're stationed along the border, I'd imagine you've heard about the Indian. His name's Geronimo."

"I know the name, *sí*." Mercado nodded.

"So you see, we got a good right to be here, whether this place is in Arizona Territory or Mexico. And we can settle that real quick just by looking at a map."

For the first time the rurale failed to meet Longarm's eyes squarely. He hesitated for a moment, then replied, "Perhaps such a treep weel not be necessary, *señor*, now that I know you are een pursuit of *un fugitivo*."

Longarm was almost sure now that his guess about the location of the border had been right. He said, "I guess the best thing to do is haul you and your crew up to Fort Huachuca. They got all sorts of maps there. Then if we can't settle things we'll just have to get the pen pushers busy in Washington and Mexico City and see which of us is right."

For a long moment the rurale stood silent. Then he asked, "We are civilized *gente,* no?"

"I reckon you could say that," Longarm agreed.

"And *gente* settle *diferencias* between theemselves, ees eet not so?"

Keeping his best poker face, Longarm nodded and replied, "Why, that depends on what you got in mind."

"You would geev a great deal to have thees Geronimo, no?"

"I reckon it'd be worth something to us, seeing as how he's the one me and Billy's chasing after."

"Eef I could arrange for you to arrest heem, there would be no more trouble between us, ees it not so?"

"I imagine that'd depend on how much fighting we'd have to do to take him."

"I do not espeak of fighting," Mercado replied. "Not weeth Geronimo or weeth my men." He glanced around the crater and indicated the fallen rurales with a wave of his hand, then said, "Weeth thees gun you hold, you have killed too many of my rurales already."

"They could've surrendered," Vail put in quickly. "And I've got a pretty good idea that if we have any more trouble along the border, the State Department in Washington's going to be knocking at the door of your ambassador."

Mercado did not reply at once. Longarm and Vail stood silent, their eyes on him. After several moments had ticked away, the rurale said, "If you breeng in Geronimo, there would be no more trouble between us, ees eet not so?"

"We sure wouldn't start nothing," Longarm replied. "Matter of fact, we'd be right sure to give your outfit some credit for helping us."

"No, no, *señor*," Mercado protested. "I would not want you to mention us. My *comandante* might not on-destan."

Longarm and Vail exchanged quick glances, then Longarm asked, "I reckon you got a pretty good idea where Geronimo might be holed up?"

Mercado nodded, then said quickly, "But I must have your word, *en fe de honra*, that you do not mention *los rurales* wheen you return heem."

"You got it," Longarm nodded. "Now all that's left to settle things up is for you to take us to wherever he's at."

"That weel be easy, *señor*." For the first time since they'd begun talking, Mercado smiled. "Come weeth me."

Longarm and Vail followed the rurale as he pushed through the silent solemn bunches of his men, who had been watching the trio while they talked. Mercado led them up the winding path that had been cut up the crater's wall. They passed the huts and caverns that the rurales had been occupying and were very near the top of the crater when Mercado stopped at a wide door of thick heavy planks that was secured by an oversized padlock.

Mercado took a key from his pocket and opened the padlock, then pulled the door open. Looking past him, ignoring the rush of warm fetid air that swept through the darkness beyond the door, Longarm and Vail could see human forms inside the cavern.

"Geronimo!" Mercado called. *"Ventá 'ca! Hay mariscales de los Estados Unidos quien vuelve a su tierra."*

For a moment nothing happened, then the form of a man seemed to materialize from the gloom. He was of medium height, and wore a loose, badly stained pullover jacket and cotton duck trousers. His feet were clad in moccasins, and a narrow headband confined his black, shoulder-length hair. As he stepped into the light he began blinking, quick successive twitches of his eyelids. He stopped the fluttering with his eyelids closed, but opened them after a moment and stared at the group standing in front of the massive opened door.

Longarm thought that he'd never before seen such black, opaque eyes before, even on another Indian. He kept his own eyes fixed on those of the man staring at him. Neither seemed inclined to blink first, but in the end it was the Indian who did so. Even then Longarm did not end his steady gaze.

"You better tell me your name," he said to the Indian.

"You know me now. Geronimo, chief of the Apache tribe."

Longarm nodded. "I sorta figured it," he said. "My name's Long, Custis Long."

"Habla español?" Geronimo asked. *"No entiendo algun mas inglés."*

Longarm looked at Billy Vail, who shook his head. Longarm motioned for him to join the colloquy and he came up to stand with the pair. Geronimo turned and shouted a few words in his own tongue and a young man came hesitantly forward from the black depths. He could have been an Apache or a Mexican. He advanced to Geronimo's side and the Apache chief said something to him in the harsh gutturals of the Apache tongue. The young man turned to Longarm.

"Con su permiso, señor, I weel put Geronimo's words een the *inglés,"* he said.

Though Longarm had no wish for the arrangement, he had no alternative. He nodded and said, "Tell him I'm a deputy United States marshal and I'm working for the Indian Bureau right now. My job's to take Geronimo and all the rest of you back to Fort Huachuca."

Nodding, the young man rattled off a volley of guttural Apache, to which Geronimo replied in kind. To Longarm, their exchange, which seemed to be made up of short one- and two-syllable words, seemed chiefly composed of gutturals and grunts. While they were talking, Vail whispered to Longarm, "Hell, I won't be any use to you, Long. That's Apache they're talking, not Spanish."

"I know that," Longarm replied. "But they don't know whether you savvy their lingo or not. I figure they'll think you do, and maybe that'll keep 'em honest."

By this time the young interpreter and Geronimo had finished their conversation. The youth turned back to Longarm and said, "He wants to know what eet was, so much the eshooting."

Longarm started to reply, but an idea struck him before he began to speak. He raised the repeating gun and fired a short burst through the open top of the dead volcano's cone.

His demonstration brought another explosive burst from the Apache, then the youth asked Longarm, "There was shots you made before? You fight rurales?"

Longarm nodded. Then he said, "Tell Geronimo me and my friend have come to take him back to Fort Huachuca. The rurales have turned him over to us. We'll guarantee to deliver him safe and sound, along with

183

whoever else from the Apache tribe is with him. You might tell him General Crook ain't there no more, and General Miles is in charge. He's not going to hurt you Apaches, all you got to do is come in peaceful."

Again the young man and Geronimo had a lengthy exchange, then the lad faced Longarm again.

"You weel take Geronimo and all that remain of us from the rurales?" he asked.

"That's the general idea," Longarm replied. "You can go quiet and peaceful, or hog-tied on mules, but you're going with us back to Fort Huachuca, dead or alive. Don't make no mistake about that."

When the interpreter spoke to Geronimo this time, the Apache chief did not reply until he'd studied Longarm from the soles of his boots to the flat-top crease of his wide-brimmed hat. Then he dropped his gaze to lock eyes with Longarm. When he found that he could not outstare him, he nodded.

"We go with you," Geronimo said. Longarm managed to keep from showing his surprise and nodded agreement. The Apache went on, "Take all Apache people?"

"Sure," Longarm replied unhesitatingly. "If you'll promise me that they won't start no ruckus."

Geronimo nodded and said, "I say peace, they go peace."

He turned and shouted in his native tongue. Longarm's eyes opened wide when he saw the ragtag group that straggled from the cave. They moved slowly, blinking even in the subdued light of the crater. Two young Apaches, barely past boyhood, emerged first. Behind them came a woman, and following her were a half-dozen men. All of them looked famished, and all wore little more than rags and tatters.

Longarm turned back to Geronimo and asked, "That's all you got left?" When the Apache nodded without changing his expression, Longarm said, "All right." Looking at Mercado he said, "I guess the rurales have got enough spare horses so all of you can ride."

Mercado frowned, then he said through compressed lips, "We do. *Gracias a tu,* Marshal Long. It weel be a while before we forget you, be esure of that!"

"Well, you tend to getting the horses ready," Longarm replied. "Billy and me will see to the rest." Then, under his breath, he said to Vail, "It looks like we got our job finished up, so you and me can be heading back to Denver pretty soon. But I'll tell you one thing for sure, Billy. I'd give a pretty penny to read what General Miles says when he makes his report to Washington!"